W9-BSS-154

Wolf Shadows

Other Books by Mary Casanova
Published by the University of Minnesota Press

Frozen

Moose Tracks

Wolf Shadows

To Alex,
Enjoy the adventure!

MARY CASANOVA

[signature]

2015

University of Minnesota Press

Minneapolis

The Fesler–Lampert Minnesota Heritage Book Series
Funded by the John K. and Elise Lampert Fund and Elizabeth and the late
David Fesler, the Fesler–Lampert Minnesota Heritage Book Series publishes
significant books that contribute to an understanding and appreciation of
Minnesota and the Upper Midwest.

Originally published in 1997 by Hyperion Books for Children
First University of Minnesota Press edition, 2013

Copyright 1997 by Mary Casanova

Mary Casanova asserts her right to be identified as the Proprietor of this work.

All rights reserved. No part of this publication may be reproduced, stored in
a retrieval system, or transmitted, in any form or by any means, electronic,
mechanical, photocopying, recording, or otherwise, without the prior written
permission of the publisher.

Published by the University of Minnesota Press
111 Third Avenue South, Suite 290
Minneapolis, MN 55401-2520
http://www.upress.umn.edu

Library of Congress Cataloging-in-Publication Data
Casanova, Mary.
Wolf shadows / Mary Casanova. — First University of Minnesota Press edition.
(The Fesler–Lampert Minnesota Heritage Book Series)
Summary: When his best friend illegally shoots a wolf while hunting in
northern Minnesota, twelve-year-old Seth struggles to determine whether their
friendship can survive their different ideas.
ISBN 978-0-8166-9031-2 (pb)
[1. Friendship—Fiction. 2. Hunting—Fiction. 3. Wolves—Fiction.] I. Title.
PZ7.C266Wo 2013   2013022807

Printed in the United States of America on acid-free paper

The University of Minnesota is an equal-opportunity educator and employer.

20 19 18 17 16 15 14 13   10 9 8 7 6 5 4 3 2 1

For Eric

I'm grateful for the expertise of Kathy Anderson, zoo-keeper of the moose (I loved getting to know Willow, Nah Nah, and Gilly), and Nick Reindl, North Trail Curator, Minnesota Zoo; Lloyd Steen and Dave Rorem, northern Minnesota game wardens; Shirley and Jerry Maertin, who raised orphaned moose; Dr. Wayne Has-bargen, Rainy River Veterinary Clinic; David Mech, renowned wolf researcher; Bill Paul, wolf biologist, Animal Damage Control, U.S. Department of Agricul-ture; Jim Schaberl, biologist, Voyageurs National Park; the wolves and staff of the International Wolf Center, Ely, Minnesota; and the resources of the Timber Wolf Alliance, Ashland, Wisconsin.

Chapter 1

Seth Jacobson froze, balanced between the third and fourth boards nailed to the tree. Tingles shot up the back of his neck. A rustling sound, a brief change in the flickering greenish gray light—that was all. Something was out there, hidden by cedar and black spruce.

"What's the matter?" asked Matt, looking up. A year older and an inch taller, he waited below the deer stand in his bright orange hunting jacket and hat.

Seth stared into the trees, looking for the slightest movement in shadows. He sensed eyes watching him. On the breeze, a sharp, pungent odor wafted to his nose. He suddenly felt like wolf bait. "The deer scent," he said, sniffing. "We reek!"

"That's the idea," said Matt.

The opening of deer hunting was two days away, and

as a trial run, they'd doused their jackets with "Bag-A-Buck" scent. Without guns, they'd waited over an hour in the stand for a deer to approach. None had.

Seth finished climbing down the stand, a narrow wooden platform built between three balsam trees and camouflaged with boughs; it rose above a deer path littered with droppings. "Nothing wrong with keeping it to yourself," Dad had said, "since you built it." But Seth wanted to share it with his best friend.

He dropped to the ground. "Remember that guy by Beaver Pass?"

Matt picked up a pinecone, wound up, hit a tree. "Yeah, the guy was attacked by a wolf, ripped apart. Needed a few hundred stitches."

"No, not exactly," Seth said. "My dad said the wolf knocked the guy to the ground, then took off. The guy was drenched with scent. The wolf probably thought he was a deer."

Matt looked at him, brown eyes unblinking. "So?"

From the ragged top of a dead pine, something swooped down. Seth flinched, but it was only a great gray owl, massive wings skimming the thin layer of snow. Silently it vanished through leafless birch trees, a mouse clamped in its talons. Had he felt the owl watching them? Was that all?

"I'm just saying," he continued, glancing around, "maybe we overdid the scent, that's all. The directions said a few drops, not half a bottle!"

"Gutless Wonder," Matt said, dark eyebrows raised. "That's what I'm gonna start calling you."

Why did Matt always seem to get the upper hand? Whenever they were together, it was as if he had to stay on top, be a notch higher somehow.

"Hey," Seth said. "I'm not gutless, it's just . . ."

"Gutless."

"Okay then, Brain-Dead." Seth crossed his arms, met Matt's stare-down. "You want to lead the way home?"

"Uh . . . truce. I don't know this part of the woods like you do." He glanced over his shoulder. "And I'm sure not sleepin' out here."

The sun slipped below the horizon, stealing the last slivers of light, as Seth started down the deer path into a rocky bowl. He picked up his pace. Matt was right. He knew this part of the woods well, but without a flashlight or compass, they could still get lost. Matt spent his days at Great Falls Junior High, but Seth usually finished his home school studies early and was in the woods by two o'clock. Seth rambled, finding tracks: moose, deer, black bear, pine marten, fox, and in the last year . . . wolf. Twice in the last month, he'd woken to howling.

They climbed a bank, then skirted the east ridge of Mackenzie Lake, which was sheeted with thin ice. A breeze rushed through the pines. Was he really gutless? Not tough enough? He had to admit, he was worried. Matt got a deer last year, but this was Seth's first season. When the moment came, could he shoot? He wasn't sure he could or wanted to, but now that he was twelve, he wanted to find out.

Rounding a snow-topped boulder, Seth jolted to a stop.

Matt slammed into his back. "What?"

Seth held up his hand and focused on listening harder, seeing more deeply.

An eerie creaking rose from behind them. He spun around. A fallen birch tree, caught in the crook of another birch, whined in the breeze. Nothing. It was nothing.

"What's with you?" Matt said.

Seth forced his shoulders back, started again. He

didn't say a word. Maybe it was his imagination working overtime. As he walked through the tall pines, he yanked a cluster of needles off a branch, held them to his nose, and breathed in the spiced air.

There.

From the corners of his eyes he saw it—movement on both sides of him. Flashes of dark, long, sleek bodies. Ghostlike. There and gone. He and Matt were a long way from home, with darkness overtaking them. "We're not alone," he whispered.

"What do ya mean?" Matt's voice jumped high.

Beneath his ribs Seth's heart drummed like partridge wings. He couldn't prove it, couldn't see anything now. His throat tightened. "Wolves."

"Oh great," Matt said, eyes darting left and right. He quickly zipped up the last few inches on his jacket, as if to protect his neck.

Seth's gut shrank into a cold, hard ball. He ground his leather boot into the earth and spoke through clamped teeth, "I told you. You never listen to me."

"What do we do?" Matt whispered. "Run for it?"

Every cell in Seth's body screamed "flee," but if the wolves were out there, running might give them reason to chase. Chalky fear climbed in his throat. "No," he said, and started off, walking faster and faster.

Nearly a half hour later, yards ahead of where the four-wheeler trail met the edge of Seth's pasture, Seth spotted a low, tawny mound. Three ravens lifted from the carcass, croaking, and flapped up to bare branches.

Seth slowed down. Whatever it was, it hadn't been there on their way into the woods. He stepped closer, a trembling sensation growing in his stomach.

A young doe—its tongue draped on the snow, black nose missing—lay crumpled, deathly still. A fresh kill. The hind section of its body was ripped open. The wolves must have eaten the doe's intestines first, leaving a deep cavity. Seth swallowed hard.

"Stealing our deer," Matt said, spitting out the words. He shook his head. "My dad always says, 'The only good wolf is a dead wolf.' Now I know why."

"Stealing? But . . ." Seth stopped beside the lifeless doe, unable to look away. "They need to eat, don't they?"

"Come on," Matt said with a groan. "Don't tell me you're a wolf lover."

"I just think . . ." Seth strained to see into the dark undergrowth. Where were the wolves now? Watching them, waiting to return to their kill site? His pulse quick-ened. "The way we smell," he said, spinning away.

"Yeah," Matt agreed, voice strained, "let's get outta here."

Instinctively, the boys broke into a run. Legs and arms pumping beneath layers of clothing, they sped down the last stretch of dark trail. Branches slapped Seth's face, and within minutes he sprang from the woods, Matt hard at his heels.

Seth raced between the split rail fence and crab apple orchard to the red barn, fumbled with the latch, and rushed inside. As soon as Matt was in, he closed the door and leaned against it, chest heaving.

Chapter 2

Seth caught himself, saw himself as if from a distance, leaning like a frightened child against the closed door. What an idiot! Did he think wolves were like the one in "Little Red Riding Hood" and could lift the latch?

He reached for the cord and flicked on the light.

"They got to you, didn't they?" Matt said from the hay bales. The corners of his mouth twitched, then he laughed.

Girls at school called Matt on the phone all the time (especially after he dumped his glasses for contacts), and it was pretty easy to understand why. Not only was he a quarterback, but he always stayed cool, controlled—well, not always.

"No . . . ," Seth said. "Just spooked me a little, that's all. Admit it, you got a little scared, too."

"Nah," Matt said, picking up a piece of green hay and clamping it between his teeth.

Seth's quarter horse, Quest, lifted his reddish brown head over the first box stall and blew air from his pink-lined nostrils.

"Hey, fella," Seth said, feeling supremely stupid now in the barn's soft light. His father was a game warden, a conservation officer, after all; he should know wolves don't attack people. Or was it that no shred of human evidence had ever been found? With a shiver, he pushed away the images of wolves and the lifeless deer and breathed in the comforting smells of hay, salty horse sweat, manure, and molasses-scented oats.

He forced himself to calm down, to get rid of his jumpiness, and walked over to Quest. "Too bad you're going to have to spend the next few weeks inside," he said, scratching under his horse's green halter. "Some trigger-happy hunter might mistake you for a deer."

"We have to keep the cows close to the barn, too," Matt said, the hay between his lips flicking up and down like a cigarette.

Seth stepped to the next stall to check on the orphaned moose calf he'd rescued from the frozen creek a

9

week ago. Injured by poachers, it had improved steadily, day by day.

Seth leaned over the stall rail. "Hi, Fudge."

The calf lifted its head, stretched out its front legs, then rose slowly and shook its scraggly coat. With only a faint limp, the calf circled the wood-sided box stall. The gunshot wound on the calf's rear hindquarter was shaved. He remembered how the vet had cleaned the wound, where a bullet had skimmed muscle, and stitched it with a short railroad track of black stitches. "When the stitches dissolve," she'd said, "you should be able to let him go."

"What about wolves?" Seth had asked, hoping that his family could keep the calf through the winter, maybe longer. At least until it could defend itself.

The vet paused and looked up from under feathery bangs, one hand on the tranquilized calf. "Sometimes, Seth, you've got to let go and let nature take its course."

Right. The image of the freshly killed deer forced its way to his mind. Easy for her to say. He grabbed a cedar branch from the pile he'd cut earlier that morning and extended it toward the moose. "Here you go."

The half-year-old calf was nearly as tall as Quest. Its

ears, lined a light brown, were as big as a mule's. Unlike an adult moose's long head, its short head almost reminded Seth of the Arabians he'd seen at horse shows. The calf stretched its neck toward the green cedar. A small triangle of bare skin decorated its muzzle. With rubbery lips, the calf pulled the nubby leaves into its mouth.

"That's right, fella," Seth said, dropping more branches into the trough.

But the calf stopped nibbling, edged itself into the corner, and like an abandoned lamb, bleated sharply.

Seth shrugged. "Something about being penned up—he just doesn't care for it. Maybe with time . . ."

Matt tossed his piece of hay into the stall. "I don't see why you can't keep him as a pet," he said. "I mean, can't you just see it, you and me"—he stretched his arms wide as if to a grateful audience—"riding a tame bull moose down Main Street?"

"It's against the law, that's why," Seth said.

"Riding a moose? Come on."

"No." Seth rolled his eyes. "*Keeping* a moose. If my dad weren't a game warden, I couldn't have him here."

"If you let him go," Matt said, his smile fading, "the

wolves will just make a quick meal of him. I'd rather starve to death than be dragged down by wolves."

Seth's stomach twisted. The idea of wolves pulling Fudge down was too much. He'd struggled to save the moose calf; he wasn't about to let it go that easily. When the calf was at its weakest, Seth had asked Matt for help. Matt brought over a bottle of warmed evaporated milk, same as he'd used with his cattle. Next, Seth took his mom's advice and called the Minnesota Zoo; a zookeeper told him where he could order special moose food. The large Purina pellets—made of corn, grains, and ground wood—looked about as appetizing as wood chips, but Fudge loved them.

The calf dropped to its front legs, lowered itself, and chewed.

Matt jutted out his lower lip, the way he did when he was thinking, which wasn't all that often. "He's ruminating, just like a cow."

"He's what?" For once, Matt had him stumped.

"You know, he has four stomachs and keeps rechewing his food." Matt nodded to himself. "He's neat. You should try to keep him."

The moose stared with earth brown eyes.

Turning away, Seth let out a slow breath. "I gotta go," he said, running his hand along Quest's stall. "I'm probably late for dinner."

As they left the barn, the automatic floodlight tripped on, cutting a swath of sparkling snow out of darkness.

"See ya," Seth said.

"Later," Matt called as he jogged toward his house across the road.

Seth stepped on the deck and reached for the door of his farmhouse. He still felt stupid about how he'd overreacted, racing back from the wolf kill to the barn. Even so, he couldn't help himself. He glanced over his shoulder and scanned the black shadows—shadows that stretched north into endless wilderness—just in case yellow eyes were glowing back.

Chapter 3

"Hey, Dad!" Seth called, stepping in. "We found a fresh—" He stopped. Mom's paperwork was scattered across the table.

Dad—still in his tan shirt and forest green pants—held the phone to his head of short blond hair and pulled at the skin of his neck. "I don't know, they're coming every two-and-a-half minutes, and they're harder, too. Water broke a minute ago." He licked his lips like a nervous young boy. "You bet. We'll be there. Fifteen minutes or *less.*"

A moan—as if his mother were in real pain—coursed down the hallway to the kitchen and hit Seth's stomach. He didn't bother to take off his boots. They'd discussed the whole thing a few days ago. When the time came, he was to go to the hospital, too. Part of the family. He didn't have to be in the delivery room (as if he wanted to be), but Mom wanted him nearby. Heck, maybe he could smoke a cigar in the waiting room while Dad coached his mother on how to breathe. How to get through the pain. Problem was, the baby was coming too early.

Next to a humming row of snack machines, Seth leaned back in a plastic chair and tilted the can of 7 Up. It fizzed down his throat. His day-old sister, Lizzy—Elizabeth Ann Jacobson—a bundle of red skin, pink flannel, and fuzzy dark hair just like Mom's, waited in a plastic bubble on the second-floor Maternity Unit. Lizzy was still in the oxygen tent, and Seth had only watched her from behind the glass wall. Now he waited alone. The doctor, Dad had said, would give an updated report soon. But that was more than a half hour ago.

At another table, two men hovered over cups of coffee.

"It's gonna be a tough season," complained the man with wire glasses. "Last winter the snow was so deep, lasted so blasted long, we lost a third of the deer! No doe licenses—not one issued this year. Can't believe it."

Deer hunting season, tomorrow. Seth didn't care if it was bucks only, but why did his sister have to be born now—three weeks early? He'd tried to hide his disappointment on the ride in. "Can't it wait?" he'd blurted, as if Mom had any control over the situation. It was a stupid thing to say. Still, he'd looked forward to getting up at dawn with Dad and going out on the first day of deer season. And Dad had actually found someone to cover for him, even though it was his busiest time of year. They'd head out together, Dad to his stand, Seth and Matt to theirs. Now everything was up in the air.

"You know," said the second hunter, wisps of hair combed over his balding head, "I saw a deer grazing on the side of the road last April. I tell ya, she was skin and bones. Bet the wolves had an easy time of it last winter, especially when the snow turned crusty. The deer break through, but wolves, they just pad over the top." He demonstrated with the flat of his hands.

What would a thriving wolf population mean for Fudge if Seth released him? Dad assured him that wolves prefer going after deer, but with the deer population down, and without the calf's mother to defend it, to flail at the wolves with her sharp hooves, Fudge was probably doomed.

"Know what I'm gonna do?" said the first hunter.

"What?"

The man lowered his voice. "Shoot the first wolf that comes along with a belly full of shot, that's what. Those are *our* deer out there."

Seth glanced up. Was he serious? Dad would want to know about this conversation. He'd set them straight. Wolves were on the "endangered species" list in every state except Alaska and Minnesota, where they were considered "threatened." Still, shooting a threatened species meant a fine of thousands of dollars and jail time. Didn't they know that?

"Know what works better?" said the balding man. "Bait a treble hook, hang it from a sturdy branch, and let 'em snap for it."

Seth's anger flared. What kind of hunters were these guys? Didn't they have any respect for the woods at all? He lifted his can to his mouth, drank it down, then slowly squeezed the can in his fist.

The balding hunter chuckled, then continued, voice lowered. "Even better, give them the doctor's orders."

"What's that?"

The man reached into his orange jacket pocket, glancing over his shoulder.

Seth pretended to study his can.

The man edged a four-inch spring onto the table and squeezed it between his thumb and third finger. "A guy ties this with string," he whispered, "freezes it, hides it in a juicy chunk of venison and leaves it out on the trail. The wolf gobbles it up, and when the string dissolves in his stomach, the spring pops open. Doubles 'em over," the man said, "and they die nice and slow."

Seth couldn't stand what he was hearing. He cleared his throat, shifted in his chair. Dad needed to know. Should he leave, go upstairs and find him? If he left, the hunters might be gone when he returned. Maybe it was better to stay, to find out all he could.

"Hey, don't show Wally that thing." The hunter pushed his glasses to the bridge of his nose. "He's sort of a wolf lover, y'know."

Seth's stomach burned. *Wolf lover*. Matt's words. Yesterday, wolves had triggered something inside of him—a gut reaction, a deep instinctive fear—but that didn't make him want to kill them.

18

Seth fumbled in his bag of cheddar chips, trying to look unconcerned.

He'd learned his own lesson. Killing a rabbit for its foot just to prove something to Matt was the most stupid thing he'd ever done. He'd vowed that he wouldn't kill anything unless his family was going to eat it.

A man, gangly as a scarecrow, walked up to the hunters' table.

"Hey, Wally. What'd they find out?"

"Indigestion," the man said, fumbling his orange cap between thickly veined hands. "Heart's tickin' like a clock."

"Bet you were just trying to get out of tonight's poker game," said the balding man, smiling, his hand on the third hunter's shoulder. "That's it, isn't it?"

Seth watched the three men walk out and turn left toward the hospital's entrance. He jumped up. If he could find his dad before they drove off . . .

A tap on his shoulder. He spun around, meeting Dad's eyes.

"Good, you're here," Seth blurted. "Did you see those guys that just left, they were talking about—"

"Lizzy needs to go to Duluth," Dad said, "by ambulance."

Spidery lines formed at the corners of his mouth. "They have a neonatal unit there—state of the art. She just came a little early, that's all, and they want to keep a good eye on her."

Neonatal unit. Duluth. Seth tried to focus on the words. His sister—his very own sister. He didn't even know her, hadn't held her yet, and still, like a red light, a question flashed: Was she going to die?

"She's going to be fine," Dad said, as if reading his mind. His hand ran to his neck. "Dr. Antonio said she's a real fighter."

Seth's thoughts jammed up like bumper cars. The hunters. Wolves. This wasn't the time. It was clear Dad had more than enough to worry about. "Um, who's gonna take care of . . ." Fudge, he wanted to say, but didn't, ". . . the animals?"

"Seth," Dad began, "I just called down there, spoke with a nurse, and she sort of . . . well . . . she sort of discouraged having siblings there."

Siblings. He wasn't used to the word.

"She said there's not much for you to do there," his dad continued, "and there's the increased risk of exposing the babies to more germs. Your mom and I want you with us, of course, but maybe the nurse is right. Let's give it a few days, see how Lizzy's doin', then I can drive back and bring you down to visit. For now, if you stay with the Schultzes, then you can just walk home to take care of the animals."

Seth stared at the squashed pop can.

Dad squeezed Seth's shoulder, once, then twice. "Don't worry," he said, trying to smile. "She'll pull through."

Chapter 4

Seth sliced two apples, three bananas, and a head of lettuce into an empty ice-cream bucket, then set it on the kitchen table. He glanced around. Dishes were still on the counter from the lunch he and Dad shared. Seth would clean up . . . later. A note scribbled on lined yellow paper lay on the table. Seth picked it up and read it a second time:

> *Seth,*
>
> *We'll be at St. Luke's Hospital, hopefully not for long. I'm sure they'll be able to help little Lizzy. If you get any messages on the answering machine, contact Ray Kruppa. He'll be filling in for me. . . .*
>
> *You're a trooper. Thanks for holding down the fort while we're away. Have a good time at Matt's.*
>
> *Lots of love,*
> *Dad*

The grandfather clock, which his father had made, ticked rhythmically, then bonged—four in the afternoon. Four. The hour Dad had recommended heading back from their stands. If they'd gone hunting, that is.

Sunlight slanted low across the living room. From his bedroom down the hall, his aquarium bubbled softly, keeping the water clear for his angelfish. Next to the dark and empty fireplace, Midnight, a ball of black cat fur, lay in Mom's teal chair.

Seth felt strangely alone.

Not that he'd never been alone before. But somehow, with his parents and Lizzy gone (having a sister was still unreal), he felt like the moose calf—orphaned.

He put on his jacket and red wool cap, grabbed the bucket, and headed for the barn. Snow melted on the deck, leaving patches of brown wood, but there would be more months of winter before a real thaw came.

Inside the barn, Quest pawed at straw, then turned to his wooden trough and chewed on its edge. A bad habit: Quest cribbed when he was bored. Bored. That's what Seth was going to be. His parents had left so quickly, there hadn't been time to talk about hunting. It was clear he wouldn't be going.

"Sorry you can't get outside," Seth said to his horse, "but there's some crazy hunters out there. They see what they want to see."

The two hunters at the hospital, for instance; they saw wolves as their enemy. Heck, they'd probably think Quest was a trophy deer. If hunters really wanted a healthy deer population, the wolf was part of that picture; they went after the frail and weak, keeping herds healthy. He'd heard stories from Hannah, his cousin in Eagan, about fat deer overrunning suburban backyards, destroying gardens. She didn't want to see her backyard deer shot or trapped, but admitted they were a growing problem.

A rustling of straw came from the second stall. Slowly, Seth stepped closer, not wanting to startle the calf. It was standing against the far wall—*shurrr, shurrr, shurrr*—scraping its flank against boards.

"Ticks, huh?" Seth asked. Winter ticks crawled up on plants in the fall, grabbed a ride when a moose walked past, then burrowed their heads into the moose's skin, sucking blood. Researchers had found thousands and thousands of ticks on dead moose. Trying to rid themselves of ticks, moose sometimes died from rubbing too much fur from their skin.

"If you let me tame you," Seth said, "maybe I can help." He wrinkled up his nose. "I hate ticks." Once, he removed thirty-three wood ticks from his old cocker spaniel, after one of Max's runs through the woods. Another time, a full tick dropped from Max onto the kitchen floor; Seth's mom stepped on it—pop!—making a red mess on the white tile.

Seth lowered the bucket of fruit and lettuce into the box stall. The calf stopped rubbing and eyed the bucket. Then it turned a circle and, with a flick of its ears, started rubbing its other flank against the wall. Where it had rubbed, two lines of exposed skin appeared. It was hurting itself on something sharp!

Without thinking, Seth stepped into the stall toward the calf. The calf backed itself into the opposite corner, long ears flattened. Its breath came in short blasts, nostrils wide.

"Don't worry," Seth said, watching the calf and running his hand over the wood-framed wall. "I'm not gonna hurt you."

His palm hit a sharp point. "Ouch." He quickly examined the blunt end of a rusty nail. Now what? Would the calf need a tetanus shot? "We better take care of this," he said, keeping an eye on the calf. Its hooves, though not as large as an adult's, were still splayed and pointed. Seth hoped the calf wouldn't use them.

He inched toward the stall door, slipped out, and found a hammer. Then he eased back in and tapped the nail flush with the board. With each pound, the moose flinched, legs shuffling, as if ready to spring over the walls.

"There," Seth said, hammer at his side, "scratch away."

The calf stared at him, its long top lashes and darker hair around its eyes giving it a sad, lonely expression.

"Listen, if I keep you in here," Seth said, "then you'll be safe. . . ." He pointed to the wide door that led to the enclosed pasture. "If I set you free, then . . . well, who knows. . . ."

He wished Fudge could talk, could tell him what to do. If he followed his father's advice, he shouldn't let himself even think about the calf. Better to not get too attached. But he wanted to help. What was wrong with that? The ice-cream bucket sat untouched. "Eat up, Fudge," Seth said, then left the stall.

He refilled Quest's water bucket, shoveled out old straw and steaming horse dung, then began brushing Quest's thick winter coat with the toothed curry comb. Quest chewed, lifting his head every other minute from his hay to look toward the calf.

As Seth pushed the blue wheelbarrow toward the pasture door, he paused. Smacking sounds came from Fudge's stall. Seth snuck a glance at the moose, eating from the ice-cream bucket. He smiled to himself.

Opening wide the door, he pushed the straw and manure-filled wheelbarrow outside and emptied it onto the growing brown mound, which would eventually become fertilizer for Mom's gardens.

Turning back to the barn, Seth heard a distant howl. He stopped abruptly.

The song started low, a single voice rising, then was quickly joined by a chorus of high-pitched and throatier howls. A pack. The song rose and fell, undulating, traveling over the treetops.

Seth scanned the woods, a jagged wall of black against the low sun. Pines on the southwest fence line cast spiny shapes across the pasture. The howling grew eerily louder—piercing—then as suddenly as it had started, it stopped.

In the silence, a tremble climbed from Seth's tailbone to his teeth.

Chapter 5

A large antlered buck, a Canada goose, and a bear hide decorated the pine walls of the Schultzes' family room. Seth glanced at the bear's white teeth and pink plastic tongue, then turned back to study the red-and-black checkerboard.

Matt was ahead by three chips. Seth was cornered, down to one.

"You're sunk," Matt said, stretching back in his navy sweater, hands clasped behind waves of brown hair. "Give it up."

"Matthew!" Mrs. Schultz called down the stairs, her voice raspy. "It's already dark out. Night before deer opener, the station is going to be swamped. Dad won't be back until after ten." The Schultzes owned the Stop and Go in town.

"Okay," Matt called back.

"Get those cows in now," Mrs. Schultz continued. "Don't keep putting it off."

"Okay, okay."

Seth looked at the checkerboard and shook his head. "Looks like it's a draw."

"A draw?" Matt said, standing. "I won and you know it. C'mon. I better go."

The Schultzes' house smelled new. Two years back they bulldozed down the old house and built a two-story log home.

Matt headed up the shiny wooden stairs from the basement, and Seth followed, slowing as he passed a wall of football photos. In more than one photo, Matt sat high on his teammates' shoulders, grinning.

Seth hustled out the back door after Matt, who was pulling on his new green-and-gold jacket. Matt hadn't lettered yet, but when you were the son of Mr. Schultz, former football player, and brother of two earlier star players at Great Falls High, you knew you'd get a letter eventually, Seth figured. It was as if you were born to play football, to be part of the team. Seth wouldn't mind trying out for football, too, but with his luck and lean build, he'd probably end up warming the bench.

Alongside the cow barn, a pole barn was stacked full with hay bales, which the Schultzes had managed to put up just days before snow fell.

Seth stepped into the metal barn after Matt. Two four-wheelers sat near the door, alongside three snow-mobiles and a trailer. The barn smelled of cows.

"I heard a wolf pack howling," Seth said, voice bouncing off the high ceiling.

Matt stopped cutting twine on a bale. "When?"

"Just before I came over," Seth said, helping toss hay into the cows' troughs, "before you got off the bus."

"Why didn't you say something earlier?"

Why hadn't he? Because he thought Matt would spout off about wolves, sounding like the two men at the hospital? Was that it? "Uh," he said. "I don't know."

Matt stepped through the corralled half of the barn, a dirt floor with a few round patches of cow dung, and opened the wide doors to the pasture. Mooing, the reddish brown cows and a handful of calves pushed inside.

"Whoa . . . slow down." Matt counted as they passed, ". . . Seventeen, eighteen, nineteen . . ."

31

He looked questioningly at Seth, who sat on the corral rail.

"The calves," Matt said. "I only count four. Where's
Star?"

Beyond the open door, a crescent moon glowed. The
temperature was plummeting. Seth rubbed his hands
together—should have worn gloves. He didn't want to
say it, but he didn't have a good feeling about this. They
needed to hurry. "Got cutters in case the calf got itself
stuck in barbed wire?" he asked.

"Yup," Matt said, hurrying to the workbench near the
door and pulling a tool from the cluttered Peg-Board. He
stuffed it into his jacket pocket and waved Seth over to a
four-wheeler.

Riding double, they set off across the Schultzes' snowy
field, beyond the barn's amber light. They bumped up and
down, running a flashlight across woods that bordered
Matt's farm, woods that turned into wilderness, stretching for miles across northern Minnesota into Canada.

Cold snuck under the back of Seth's jacket. They
crossed the wooden bridge that spanned a frozen shallow
stream, winding slowly back and forth, checking out a
mound of bare dirt here, a low bush there.

"Where is she?" Matt called, his voice nearly swallowed by the motor's roar. "She just disappeared."

Seth didn't answer.

At the north side of the pasture, well beyond view from the barn and house, the four-wheeler stopped close to a barbed-wire fence. Lights shone on the calf, lying on its side, the familiar white patch marking its dark nose.

"Star!" Matt exclaimed.

Could it still be alive? Sick or injured? Had they made it just in time? Seth clung to a thin rope of hope, but it quickly slipped from grasp. A dark ring stained the snow near the calf's belly and hindquarters.

The boys jumped off and slowly edged closer, snow crunching under their boots. Seth held the icy flashlight, swinging it over the calf's head and neck, its stiff tongue, toward its body. Just like the deer they'd found, the calf's abdomen was cleaned out. From its hindquarters, chunks of flesh were gone.

Wolf tracks surrounded the site. Tufts of reddish brown hair were scattered everywhere. The wolves must have fled abruptly, alerted by the four-wheeler lights bobbing over the field.

Matt picked up a few hairs, rubbed them between his

fingers, and swore under his breath. The headlights caught his face, eyebrows scrunched, mouth wrinkled like a raisin. He struck at the air with his fist. "Stupid wolves!" he shouted. "She was my favorite!"

Seth realized then that the calf was one of the two calves Matt had bottle-fed six times a day that summer after its mother died of pneumonia. Star probably meant to Matt what Fudge meant to him. He wanted to say he was sorry, that he really felt bad, but the words stuck in his throat.

Chapter 6

"We should string 'em up! Tack their hides to the barn!"
Matt's father boomed, thick arms braced against the edge
of the oak dining table, cards fanned in his big hands.

Sitting next to Matt, Seth popped a handful of popcorn into his mouth. He didn't have to stretch his imagination very far to know where Matt picked up some of
his ideas. He studied his hand: one ace, king, and
queen—all hearts—good cards, wrong suit. They were
playing clubs.

Nonsense, a white-faced golden retriever, shifted
under the table and lay on Seth's stocking feet.

"I don't get it," said Stubby, whose nickname matched
his stout build and weed-whacked hair. As Matt and Seth
returned from the field, a new red pickup had pulled into
the driveway. It was Matt's two older brothers, home to

hunt from St. Cloud. "I remember you hunting wolves from planes when I was little," Stubby continued.

Mr. Schultz smiled and combed his thin mustache with his fingers. "Lots of wolves. We'd just fly down above an ice-covered lake and shoot. And we got paid for doing it, too. Now that was when the laws made sense. A bounty of fifty bucks per hide." He slapped down a card. "And then, when the laws changed, someone protested by leaving a dead wolf on the steps of the county courthouse."

"Oh yeah?" Brett said. "Never heard that one." He hooked a thumb beneath his orange suspenders and ran it slowly up and down.

"I'm gonna call that Kruppa fella," Mr. Schultz said. "Get him out here first thing in the morning. The government's payin' for this one, not that four hundred bucks is nearly enough. If we can't kill wolves, then we sure better get something for our losses." He squeezed his fist. "And not like two years ago, either. What a fiasco. You can remind your dad of this, Seth—"

Seth looked up. He felt on the spot, somehow expected to cover for his father's decisions. It wasn't the first time someone was frustrated with how his father handled things. "They want to make up their own rules," Dad had said once, "even when I tell them how the laws read." No way. Seth wasn't getting himself stuck in the middle of this one.

Mr. Schultz went on, "Lost two calves, and because we couldn't find any evidence, we didn't get paid. Well, it doesn't take a rocket scientist to know what happened! Those wolves were just waiting in the woods for the cows to give birth, then they snuck right in and carried the calves away—probably before they could even get up and walk."

Matt elbowed Seth. "See?"

Seth played dumb. "What?" But he pictured the scene. Wolves waiting in dense woods, watching cows thick with pregnancy, waiting for them to drop their young—a slippery calf on unsteady legs. Weakened from giving birth, how was the mother cow suppose to defend her young? If that's what happened, then he had to admit, wolves were smart.

Stubby played a card on top of the pile, then scooped it toward himself. "Ericksons lost their dog to wolves. They came home from work and the only thing left on the chain was the collar."

Nonsense groaned beneath Seth's feet.

"Huh," Brett said, running his finger over his lower lip. "No loss. That squeaky, annoying dog? Always yipping when I jogged past it."

"Protected for too long," said Mr. Schultz with finality. "It's time to open up a hunting season on 'em, same as deer."

Seth glanced at the pile of orange hunting gear—shells, boots, and clothes—in the middle of the living room. A hunting season on wolves? Seth pondered that for a moment, lifting a can of root beer to his lips. It's not as if anyone would eat one.

Stubby dealt another round of cards.

Seth drew his cards toward him, fanned them, and regrouped them by suit. Not much better.

Mr. Schultz said, his voice growing louder, "I can't concentrate anymore." He put down his cards. "This makes a lousy end to a bad week. First, we nearly had the football season in the bag—then Matt got his leg all bruised up and crawls to bed with a sore throat." He glanced toward Matt.

Matt grabbed a handful of popcorn and crammed the whole thing in his mouth, focusing on his cards. He'd been mostly silent since they returned to the house with the bad news.

"When I was his age, I got the flu, threw up during halftime, then went right back out there." He looked at Brett and Stubby. "And you guys, you didn't let nothin' get in your way. That's how you earned those scholarships." He paused, shooting Matt a glance. "Y'know, Matt, you could learn a little something from your brothers. We lost—all because of a little sore throat."

Matt, his mouth stuffed like a chipmunk, glanced at Seth. His brown eyes were darker than usual, pained.

"And losing that calf," Mr. Schultz continued. "If you'd brought those cows in first thing when you got home, before it got dark outside, maybe—not that I'm blaming you—but sometimes, Matt, you could use another brick of self-discipline."

Why wouldn't he just stop? Seth thought. Hadn't he already said enough? But Mr. Schultz plowed ahead.

"Look at your brothers. Stubby's not an accountant by accident. And Brett, some thought he was washed up his freshman year, but he's still playing hard with the big boys at the U."

Finally, Brett quietly piped in. "Dad, he's still a kid. He's got lots of time to grow up."

Matt threw down his cards, jaw firm, and pushed away from the table. He motioned to Seth with his arm. "C'mon."

"Guess I'm done," Seth said, and followed his friend around the corner, down the stairs to Matt's bedroom, a jungle of dirty clothes, schoolbooks, and football gear. Seth agreed, a guy could only take so much. Besides, it was late, and he hadn't slept much in the past twenty-four hours.

Matt flopped himself on his water bed, back first, and gnawed furiously at a fingernail. "He doesn't think I can do anything right! Sometimes," he said, motioning his head toward the trombone case leaning in the corner, "I think I'd rather play in the marching band . . . see how he likes *that*."

A knock came at the bedroom door. "Good night," Mrs. Schultz said, opening the door a crack. Nonsense slipped past her pear-shaped form and jumped up on the end of Matt's bed. With a groan, he stretched out on his side.

"Seth," Mrs. Schultz said, "you know, I don't see why

you couldn't hunt tomorrow, too. As long as we're all going."

Seth looked up, surprised. "Sure." If he were hunting with adults, it had to be okay. Why hadn't he figured that out? He'd hurry home in the morning, take care of Quest and Fudge and Midnight, and then return with his license and gun.

"Stubby and Brett will want to leave at dawn, but you two could leave with us, after we deal with the wolf problem." Then she turned away.

Seth climbed into his sleeping bag and stared at the mobile of colorful NFL helmets turning slowly above him. His thoughts spun from deer hunting, to Lizzy, to Fudge, to the pool of dark red on the snow.

Finally, Matt spoke, his voice stretched like steel wire. "I'm shooting the first wolf that lays another tooth on one of our calves." His words were barbed.

Seth stopped rubbing his toes against the soft flannel lining of his sleeping bag. Matt couldn't really be serious, could he? If he were, he certainly wouldn't be talking like this to him, son of Kevin Jacobson, conservation officer. Matt was probably just blowing off steam.

"Even if the government pays," Matt said, his voice

41

softening, "money can't replace Star, y'know."

"Yeah," Seth said. "I know."

"I had hoped to show Star at the county fair this year," Matt said. "Guess I can't now, can I?"

Seth felt bad for Matt and wished he could do something, but what? Only a week ago, Matt had helped him that first night after getting the moose calf back to the barn. In the stall's back corner, the calf had lain motionless, half-dead, head drooped on the straw.

When Seth hadn't a clue what to do, Matt had suggested bottle-feeding it.

Matt had leaned against the stall, chin on crossed arms. With two hands, Seth extended the bottle of warmed milk replacer. Fudge stretched his neck slowly toward it, then pulled back, like a turtle into its shell.

"Hey, you gotta drink something," Seth pleaded. The calf didn't move. Seth let the weight of the two-quart plastic bottle pull his arms down.

"Try again," said Matt.

Seth extended the bottle.

This time, the moose calf stretched out its splayed hoofs, readying itself to stand, then lowered itself flat again. Seth studied the moose, its bony frame, its dull coat.

"Maybe he's got brain worm," Seth said, wiggling the bottle back and forth, touching the end of the calf's muzzle.

"I've heard of that. What is it?"

"Deadly, that's what," he said. "There was a moose wandering around the streets of Atikokan, completely confused."

"Don't deer pass it on to moose somehow?"

"Yeah. The parasite doesn't bother them but they pass it through their droppings, then slugs feed on the droppings, pick up the parasite, and slime their way to a nearby plant. When a moose comes along, it munches down the slug with the plant."

"Mmmmm," Matt said. "Tasty."

The calf's eyes followed the bottle as Seth passed it back and forth slowly in front of its muzzle.

Seth continued, feeling like Mr. Science. "When the parasite makes its way from the moose's stomach to its brain, the moose goes slowly crazy. Can't escape hunters—humans or wolves." The moose calf suddenly stretched its rubbery lips, gingerly tasting the milk with its tongue, then began to drink.

"Good boy," Seth said, smiling.

Like satellite dishes, the calf's ears turned toward Seth's voice. The bottle's pale milk began to flow, disappearing down the calf's smacking mouth.

A couple bottles full of warm milk, and that was all the calf needed to return to solid foods and water. Without Matt's suggestion of trying the oversized milk bottle, perhaps the calf would have never made it.

Nonsense snored softly, his head draped on the edge of the bed, his lip flapping open as he exhaled. From the floor, Seth studied the dog's mottled pink-and-black gums, its teeth badly in need of brushing. With a sudden jolt, the dog's front and hind legs twitched spastically, then stopped. Probably a squirrel dream. If Nonsense were a younger dog, he might keep wolves away.

Years back there were no fences or trespassing signs. Wolves and humans lived side by side, sharing the same game—deer, caribou, moose. Now, if a herd of cows were only a fence line away from deep woods, could the wolf be blamed for going after easy food?

Seth took a deep breath—his mind tired—and reached for the olive-colored light on Matt's nightstand. Life could be so hard to understand, he thought, before plummeting into a deep sleep.

Chapter 7

A grosbeak, red feathers puffed, landed on a swirl of Norway pine needles, pecked, then lifted into the air as the boys approached. Seth led, and Matt followed, matching footsteps in the two-inch layer of snow. The sky was muddy gray, the air an almost balmy fifteen degrees.

Seth breathed in through his nose, out through his mouth, trying to hush his own breath. In the back pocket of his orange wool pants, he carried his hunting certificate. His Buck knife was strapped to his belt in a leather sheath, and in gloved hands he carried his father's Remington rifle, angled slightly downward.

After the Schultzes learned that Kruppa couldn't investigate the wolf problem until later, they decided to head out and were in the woods by nine o'clock.

Matt's parents veered off together to hunt the east

arm of Lost Lake, to use a stand complete with two arm-chairs and windows. More of a cabin than a deer stand.

"You boys stick together," Mr. Schultz had said, "go ahead to Seth's stand, and we'll meet you back before dusk. If you get a deer, you can try to gut it, Matt, or else come and get me and I'll give you a hand. I'll get in there as close as I can with the four-wheeler if I have to."

Clusters of brown oval droppings littered the path. Deer sign. Even if they hadn't hit the woods at dawn, Seth had the feeling they were going to see some action. His pulse sped. A surge of energy filled him. He was an older brother now, and his parents had really trusted him to watch over things while they were away. If he were lucky, maybe he'd have a deer to show his parents when they returned. Venison. Yeah.

A red squirrel scurried across the arms of a birch, shrilly chattering, telling them they'd invaded its terri-tory.

"Let's take a shortcut," Seth whispered. He pointed to a beaver dam, chewed logs and sticks buttressing a mud wall between a small pond above and a creek below. On the east side of the pond, a snow-covered beaver hut, a masterfully constructed mound of sticks, rose above the layer of ice. Seth imagined a pair of beavers nestled inside, their rooms fully stocked with aspen leaves for the winter months when their young would be born. Another expanding family.

"We'll get to the stand quicker if we just walk the edge of the dam," he said quietly, looking back.

Matt nodded.

Carefully, Seth placed one foot over the other, one arm out for balance. Before the snow came, he could easily walk the dam, but now, he was less sure of his footing. He really didn't want to wipe out.

Halfway across, he stopped and squatted to look at some tracks. They were about five inches wide—much like a dog's, but bigger. "Matt," he whispered, "wolf tracks."

"Oh yeah?"

The large tracks led across the top of the dam. Seth scanned the dark shoreline of the pond, wondering if a wolf was watching them. "Maybe it was coming across the dam when it heard us approaching," he said. "Think it was after . . . nah." He wasn't going to let himself get worked up into another frenzy. He pointed to the hut, at the far edge of the pond. "Wolves eat beaver," Seth said.

47

"And sometimes, they'll den up in an abandoned beaver hut."

"Y'know, Seth, sometimes I think you're a walking encyclopedia."

Not a compliment. "Okay," Seth said. He stood up. "I'll shut up."

"No, that's okay. You just know so much, that's all."

"Comes from being home schooled," Seth said. "I'm probably not as distracted by girls," he joked, "like some guys I know."

"Maybe you need to get a little more distracted. You know, get away from the woods and home a little. Stir things up. Not be such a Nature Boy."

Though Matt's tone wasn't sarcastic, the words stung. Yet Seth knew there was some truth in them. Home schooling was mostly his mom's idea, and it had worked out pretty well, but lately, he'd found himself thinking about going back to public school. Maybe playing football next year. Seeing more kids. Making more friends. Getting more involved. But when he'd brought up the subject, she didn't seem to hear. Now, with a baby coming home soon—if Lizzy pulled through—he worried that Mom would lean on him to babysit, especially when she returned to part-time social work.

Seth walked along the top of the dam, trying not to step on the wolf tracks so Matt could see them. But his boot slipped, loosening a patch of brown earth that fell to the iced creek. He scrambled for footing, but there was nothing there. Next thing he knew, his body was falling, arms flailing. The gun flew from his grasp.

"Seth, watch out!"

But it was too late. He landed in a heap, one leg below the logs in muddy water. Cold trickled into his left boot, seeped through his wool sock. He struggled to pull his leg out, to get to the bank, before breaking through the ice completely. His gun, where was it? The walnut stock jutted up from a tangle of wood and water and snow. Seth grabbed at it, pulled it up from a thick vise of mud, and log by log, hauled himself to shore. His left ankle hurt, burned, but the cold water was quickly numbing the pain. He pulled himself up the slippery bank of the creek. As he neared the top edge, Matt held out his gloved hand. "Here," he said.

"That was stupid," Seth said, standing. He looked at his gun and groaned. Tufts of mud and weeds were crammed in the rifle's small barrel. If he tried to shoot it, would it backfire, explode? "Dang. I really mucked it up," he said, pulling off his gloves and picking at the gun.

"Got that right," Matt said, shifting back and forth in his insulated rubber boots. "Wet?"

"Left foot's soaked." Seth snapped a twig off a nearby branch. Using it as a small pick, he loosened the mud around the gun's tip and pulled at the weeds. An inch of impacted mud slipped out, free and clear.

Matt sighed.

Seth glanced up.

The corner of Matt's lip fell slightly. "Well," he said, disappointment in his voice. "We better go back. You'll freeze."

Matt's oversized orange vest and insulated orange cap looked more like they belonged on a thirty-year-old. It was as if the two of them were playing "hunters." Seth smiled, remembering the time they'd made antlers out of paper-towel tubes and turned Nonsense into a deer, then hunted him all afternoon with bows and rubber arrows. This was their first time deer hunting together. He shook his head. No, he wasn't going to wimp out over a wet foot.

"Uh-uh," Seth said. "We're too close to stop now. We follow the creek right to the lake, and then—bingo—

we're right at my stand." He felt odd, catching himself saying "bingo," the word he'd picked up from one of the hunters at the hospital.

"You're sure?" Matt's mouth turned up slightly. He reached for his .30-30, which he'd set against a birch.

"Really, I'll be fine. I'm already working up a sweat." He unzipped his jacket, pulled off his green sweater and hung it on a nearby branch, then put his jacket back on. "There. That's better."

"Yeah," Matt agreed, following Seth's actions, stripping down to a T-shirt and baggy orange sweatshirt. "I don't know why my mom insisted on so many layers.

"Hey," he asked, gun in hand again, "did you bring a rope?"

"Yup." Seth tapped his red waist pouch, the one he usually filled with waxes for cross-country skiing. Now it held a coiled length of yellow nylon rope. How they'd pull a full-grown deer through the woods, he didn't really know. One thing was certain, they'd skip the shortcut over the dam.

They followed the winding creek for about thirty yards, then set off through a dark stand of cedar to Mackenzie Lake.

The woods were still—too still. A breeze would help cover their crunching sounds and carry their human scent downwind, so deer wouldn't smell them coming.

Along the shore, Seth noticed a half-foot rut sloping down the bank. He stepped closer to investigate. Beneath an overhanging cedar and lip of land lay a small pile of clam shells. He picked one up. Crusty gray clams had been pried open, revealing silky pink insides. The meaty critters were gone. Seth looked out into the bay.

Two black openings were cut in the snow-dusted ice. Suddenly, out of one, a brown head popped up, whiskers wide, eyes staring. An otter! It hopped out onto the ice, skidded across on its belly, and just as quickly as it appeared, dove into the second hole. Seth dropped the shell, smiled, and turned to Matt.

Matt leaned against the slanted cedar tree, back to the lake. He'd missed it all.

Click. Clickety. Crack!

They stared at each other. What in the world?

Crack! Crack!

Seth stood still and followed the sound to the opposite edge of the bay. Motionless, the boys watched. The sound came from within the cedars. What was it? A bull moose? Seth remembered trying to attract one by banging sticks together.

The white tail of a deer emerged first—a buck. Rear legs straining, it was trying to hold its own against another buck. Antlers engaged, the larger buck emerged from the woods, its rack twice the size of the smaller buck, its coat grayish brown.

Click-clickety. Crack! They tapped their antlers together, them rammed harder. The larger buck lifted its front legs and thrashed with its hooves. From their black noses, shots of air sounded.

Matt slowly pulled his gun into his hands. Seth was aware of what he was doing, that this might be a once-in-a-lifetime shot, that maybe they wouldn't get another chance at two bucks. But he couldn't take his eyes off them. Off the drama, their fight for dominance. So involved they hadn't even picked up the boys' scent.

The larger deer pushed on toward the lake, and the smaller buck's legs surrendered, one step at a time, edging out on the ice, its hooves raking—*tink, tink*—for a grip. Ice cracked, and its hind legs broke through, its body going down as shafts of water and ice exploded into the air.

A circle of ravens, black and scraggly, appeared and hovered overhead, calling.

Seth hoped the deer could get footing, that the lake would be shallow there, but he knew better. Mackenzie Lake was a trout-fishing lake, nearly one hundred feet deep in spots.

Splash! The deer, its rack and head above the water, snorted and wheezed. It broke at the surrounding ice with its sharp hooves, carving a wider circle for itself.

The ravens croaked in nearby trees.

Seth glanced back toward shore. The large buck had vanished, disappeared into the cedars. His breath caught. In the buck's place, standing still on the rocky shore, eyeing the struggling deer, was a gray wolf.

Chapter 8

The wolf stood on the opposite shore, maybe twenty-five yards away. Seth didn't move. He held his breath, his heart pounding. Except for the wolf that flashed across the highway on a drive to Two Harbors, this was the first time he'd seen one in the wild. And he was relieved it was intent on the deer, not on them.

The wolf, heather gray with lighter face and leg markings, blended in with rock and snow. It reminded Seth of an oversized sled dog. Its neck fur was ruffled, revealing a black collar—a radio collar?—but its ears, snout, and legs were much larger than a husky's. Lanky, huge, lean. If it smelled them, noticed them, it would vanish.

Good thing Matt was there to see it, too; otherwise who would believe him?

A raven swooped over the deer's antlers, then up into

birch limbs. Seth had heard ravens earlier—could they have alerted the wolf to the deer's predicament?

With its tail straight out, ears straight ahead, the wolf stepped stealthily on wide paws toward the lake's edge.

Another raven swooped down from the trees, over the deer, as if testing how close the animal was to death.

Head lowered, the wolf edged onto the lake. But it was only one wolf—where were the others? One wolf couldn't bring down a deer by itself, could it? Maybe it could.

The deer's eyes went wider, showing white; its snorting grew frantic. Its front legs were on the ice, and the ice was holding. With a groan, the buck was heaving itself out of the frigid water.

In the same instant, at of the edge of Seth's vision, he saw Matt, raising his .30-30 to his shoulder. No! It wouldn't be fair to shoot the buck now. . . . If it sank in deep water, it would be a waste!

As if in slow motion, mouth open, Seth turned his head as the gun went off, blasting the air. It knocked Matt back against the cedar tree and sent a sprinkling of snow onto his contorted face.

"Got him!" Matt shouted, and with a pit in his gut,

Seth spun his gaze back, back to the ice, but the deer was out of the water, leaping through the air, front legs curled and hind legs extended. Touching the ground only once, it bounded into the woods, its white tail lifted high.

The wolf was gone, too.

Matt stood still. Then he huffed and slowly lowered his rifle. "C'mon."

"Uh . . . I think you missed," Seth said, glad the deer had escaped.

Matt didn't seem to hear. He was stepping out from under the cedar branches and heading along the shoreline to where the wolf and bucks had stood.

Seth followed, catching branches from whipping his face, as images rolled through his mind. The bucks going head to head, the wolf, and the deer's near brush with death. This time, the buck escaped.

He followed Matt over a fallen pine, circling wide around a patch of tangled brush, and within minutes they were on the opposite shore.

Then Seth saw it. On the shore where the wolf had stood, gray strands of hair and a bloodstain the size of a handprint sprayed the snow. Could Matt have . . . did he . . . ?

Matt squatted next to the blood and glanced toward the balsam trees.

"Told you I got him."

Seth couldn't answer, didn't want to speak. Saying what he thought would make it too real. His insides rolled slowly, like a fish giving way to death, belly up.

Matt didn't meet—wouldn't meet—Seth's eyes. He faced the lake, the open patch of water. Ice tinkled against ice.

Seth opened his mouth to speak, but words seemed senseless. Worthless. He spun away, disgusted, and stopped himself. He couldn't believe it! It was as if he'd just witnessed a murder. And what would happen when his dad found out, then what? Was he suppose to keep quiet, act like it never happened? Did Matt expect him to lie about it?

"You gut-shot the wolf, didn't you?!" The words exploded out of Seth's mouth.

Matt was still on his haunches, facing the lake. He didn't turn around.

"Why?!" Seth demanded.

Matt humphed. He didn't move. "You think wolves are so great, then why won't you let Fudge go, huh?"

Seth squared himself, legs planted. Hot anger churned in his chest. He didn't want to look at Matt's face or hear his lame arguments.

Matt shifted his feet and started to stand.

"Don't even try to stand up," Seth warned, clenching his fists tighter, "or I swear, I'm gonna hit you!"

Matt didn't move.

Seth swore and pivoted away, rifle in hand. "You find your own stupid way home!"

Then he took off down the shoreline, crashing through the brush. He didn't care if he scared away every deer for miles. Matt's shot had destroyed everything.

Chapter 9

At the creek, Seth grabbed his sweater from a branch and raced across the dam's length, not caring if he fell or not. Matt shot a wolf! Did he have any idea what he'd done? A threatened species could mean a fine of thousands of dollars and jail time! What in the world was he thinking? Maybe Matt wasn't an A student, but Seth had never thought he was stupid.

"I don't care if he gets lost out there," Seth muttered. Despite the chilly air, a sweat dampened his brow. If Matt couldn't find his way home, it would serve him right to spend a night in the woods. Maybe he'd learn something.

Where the deer path crossed the four-wheeler trail, Seth went left, toward home. He'd sleep there tonight. The last thing he was going to do was share a room with Matt. And that collar. Matt was in huge trouble. It had been radio-collared. What an idiot!

Eyes burning, stomach twisting, he stormed down the deer path to the main trail.

Under a towering pine, Seth paused. He stood beneath its spreading massive branches, next to bark crusted with years of green and gray lichen. Where was the timber wolf now? Limping away to escape the pain in its belly, pain that wouldn't go away until it dragged itself to a place deep in the woods to die slowly? Sure, Matt had reason to be angry about losing the calf, but that didn't mean that shooting a wolf somehow balanced the scales.

At his field, shadows stretched like gaunt soldiers. As he ran his hand along the split rail fence toward the barn, a deep ache and anger surged inside him. Tears brimmed quickly, warm and salty. He wiped them away with the back of his gloved hand, and swallowed hard. "What a brainless thing to do. . . ."

He became suddenly aware that he couldn't feel his left foot. He tried to wiggle his toes, but they didn't respond. He hurried toward his barn, its faded red shape more like home than anywhere else in the world. The noon sun was already low in the sky and hazed by thin clouds. A breeze came up suddenly and whistled through the pine boughs. Seth felt empty. Awful. His first day of deer hunting wasn't all it was cracked up to be.

He trudged to the barn and stepped in, warm air blanketing him. Quest swung his chestnut head over his stall door and rumbled a deep hello, pawing in his stall.

"Hey, Quest," he said, pulling off his gloves. From the metal garbage can he scooped a handful of molasses oats and extended his hand in front of Quest's velvety muzzle. His horse nibbled, wetting his hand with slobber.

From the moose calf's stall came the sound of rustling straw. Heck, maybe Seth would sleep in the barn tonight. And why not? Quest and Fudge made better friends than Matt could ever be. Sometimes, animals made more sense than humans.

Seth took a deep breath, panged for a second by guilt. What about his own actions? Maybe he shouldn't have abandoned Matt. Then he shook his head, and anger surged through him like white water. He could never forgive Matt for what he'd done.

Sitting on a hay bale, Seth untied his left boot. He tugged extra hard, the wet leather stiff with cold. He peeled down the red wool sock, then the white liner designed to wick away moisture. Right.

His toes were swollen balloons, white as cotton. "Not good." He pinched his big toe. Nothing. With both hands around his foot, he rubbed gently, then stopped. What had he learned about frostbite? Don't rub, wasn't that it? That the skin could rub off? And what else? Don't heat it up too fast, like by putting it in a tub of hot water.

He shivered uncontrollably.

"Huh. Maybe the barn isn't that warm." Seth looked at the wet sock and boot. If Matt had been the one to fall in the creek, Seth wouldn't have left him. But Matt was dry. He'd be fine. Seth doubted his boot would be easy to get back on, now that he'd taken it off. It was probably easier to hop to the house on one leg.

He hobbled up the deck steps and paused, hand on the back door. Light snowflakes were beginning to fall. Could he risk letting Matt get lost? Could he really? But the sound of Matt's gunshot replayed in his mind, and his stomach clenched. He hopped inside.

Midnight greeted him, snaking in and out of his legs, purring at full volume. Seth poured cat food into Midnight's bowl, then noticed the answering machine on the kitchen counter, blinking red.

He pushed the play button: "Hi, Seth. This is Mom."

Her voice sounded tired, but happy. "It seems strange," she said, "to be down here with your dad and Lizzy without you. Seems like part of the family is missing, because it is, I guess. Don't you hate leaving messages on answering machines? I sure do. They make me feel like I'm talking to a wall. But I want you to know that I'm thinking about you and hoping you're doing okay at Matt's. Oh, and Lizzy is coming along fine. She started nursing today, which is a big relief, because her little lungs had been clogged up and she was having difficulty getting air. Oh, she's so adorable, Seth. You'll just have to hold—"

Beep. The machine cut her message short.

Seth walked down the hallway and peered into the room opposite his own, hands pressed against the door frame. Wallpaper—bright blue, green, yellow, and red stripes with a border of circus elephants—splashed the walls. Mom had picked the color scheme after reading that babies prefer primary colors over pastels, such as pink and light blue. A white crib with white ruffled sheets sat waiting—empty. He still couldn't quite grasp it. A baby sister. At first he'd felt a pang of disappointment, had really hoped for a little brother. But it would be okay. Heck, he could teach her to ride horseback, to run barrels when she got older. Still, the whole thing—a sister—was weird.

Downstairs, under a green-and-black–striped wool blanket, Seth ate his trail lunch, a salami and cheese sandwich. Then he stretched out on the couch and watched part of an old western. The figures moved across the screen, but he couldn't concentrate on the story. Midnight curled into Seth's chest and, with his pink sandpaper tongue, licked Seth's wrist.

Punching the remote control, Seth zipped from one channel to the next, surfing through the whole three stations they received. Some people, like Matt, had satellite dishes with a thousand zillion stations to choose from. Matt was spoiled, especially as the youngest. Having to find his own way home was probably just what he needed.

"I hope he regrets it," Seth said, guilt nudging at him. He pushed it away, his eyes growing heavy. "Hope he pays."

His left big toe began to throb, a sign of life. At least his toes wouldn't have to be cut off.

Hours later, he woke up, rubbing his eyes. "Get your shovels ready," the five o'clock weather reporter said, his smile as wide as the Grand Canyon, "because we've got plenty of snow coming our way tonight." You'd think he'd just announced an all-expense-paid trip to Florida. "A Canadian Clipper will be blasting across the northern half of Minnesota dumping a predicted ten inches of snow before morning. That's right. You heard it. Ten inches of white stuff! Weather advisories have been issued immediately for persons traveling—"

Seth hit "off" on the remote control. He leaned his face into his fists. Dang it! With more snow, Matt couldn't even follow their tracks—if he was lost, that is. "Quit being a mother hen," Matt had said once. Maybe he was worrying too much.

He moved Midnight off his lap and onto the couch. "Sorry," he said. He stood to walk, and limped, trying to avoid putting weight on his left foot.

Hobbling up the stairs, he knew what he had to do. Go to the Schultzes'. Check if Matt had returned, which he must have by now. Seth would stand at the door and keep it short—to the point. He didn't want to waste words on that jerk.

He glanced beyond the lacy curtains on the kitchen window. Daylight was completely gone. A shiver fingered its way up his back as he sat on the wooden bench in the entry. The house was too quiet.

He eyed his foot, shook his head at the puffy pink toes, too swollen to squeeze into his own boots. He reached into the closet and pulled out Dad's Redwings, size eleven, three sizes bigger than his own. Fumbling in the socks and mittens basket, he pulled out two pairs of wool socks, slipped them on, then pulled on his father's boots. Way too big. Then, like Bigfoot, he clomped outside through a couple inches of new fluff, down the driveway, and crossed the road. He looked ridiculous, but he'd make it quick.

When Mrs. Schultz opened the front door, her smile dropped like a book off a shelf. "Where's Matt?"

"Uh . . . I was just checking to see if, uh, he'd returned yet?"

A warmth climbed to his neck, and he clenched his jaw so hard a pain shot through his left molar.

"Step in," she said, hand on his shoulder, hurrying him inside and shutting out the dark and cold. Smells of spaghetti and garlic bread tickled his nose. His stomach growled.

"Now, what's this?" Her voice was rising, charged with accusation, worry. "I thought you two were sticking together. You were both supposed to head back—before dark."

"Well . . ." He lowered his eyes. What would his father say about this? Dad would be outraged to learn that Seth had left Matt in territory he didn't know. Like water bursting over a dam, guilt overwhelmed him.

"Did he get a deer out there?" Mrs. Schultz pressed. "Is he waiting for someone to come help him?"

Brett and Stubby's voices came from the living room. "Punky got a deer?" "Sounds like it."

They'd called Matt "Punky" since Seth could remember, short for "little punk," even though Matt told them he hated it.

Mr. Schultz stepped from around the oak banister. "Heard a shot just after eleven this morning. What did he get?"

A wolf, Seth wanted to say. He got a wolf. He glanced up. "Uh . . . there were a couple of bucks—missed them." He stared at his dad's boots.

"But you were suppose to stick together," Mr. Schultz reminded him. *Stick together.* It was a rule, an order, a law of the woods that he'd violated.

Seth cleared his throat. Mr. and Mrs. Schultz had always been generous with him, for years supplying him with free pop and snacks every time he visited their

68

house. He forced himself to meet their eyes. "I was checking to see if he'd come back yet." He didn't want to worry
the Schultzes more than necessary, but he had to let them
know. "And there's a storm coming. Ten inches."

"Oh, that's just great," Mrs. Schultz said, reaching for
a gold-and-white pack of cigarettes on a lamp stand. "I
thought you two had more sense than—"

"Angel, don't," Mr. Schultz broke in. "Matt's gonna
turn up any second, probably coming this way now. But
until he gets here, Brett and Stubby and I will head out
there to find him. Seth can show us the way, can't you?"

Seth inhaled hard, but his words came out threadbare,
unconvincing. "You bet."

Chapter 10

"I'll keep the food warm," Mrs. Schultz called as they headed outside.

"There isn't quite enough snow for snowmobiling," Mr. Schultz said as Brett and Stubby trailed behind him. "Let's take the four-wheelers."

Snow puffed around their boots. Seth followed behind, glancing up at a sky void of stars. Flakes continued to fall, lightly, slowly.

"When we find him," Mr. Schultz continued, "he can ride behind in the trailer."

They rolled the two four-wheelers from the barn, and Mr. Schultz became strangely silent.

"Remember my first deer," Brett said, "how I didn't want to leave it, so I waited until you showed up?"

Mr. Schultz nodded, looking ridiculous in his

orange bomber hat, flaps tied down over his ears.

"Matt's probably out there now—a little cold, no doubt—but he's fine," Brett said casually.

Was Brett really that confident that Matt was okay? Or was he acting, trying to make things seem less serious somehow? Seth couldn't ease the knot that was tightening in his stomach. If something had happened, it would be his fault.

Blue clouds of exhaust rolled like storm clouds behind the machines. Mr. Schultz motioned for Seth to get on first. "You know where to go, Seth." Then he hopped on behind.

Stubby drove the other four-wheeler. Brett sat behind him and waved Seth on to lead the search party.

Seth gave the four-wheeler gas, lurched forward, and headed down the Schultzes' driveway, across the road, and toward the trail leading behind his house. If it were light out, he'd ride Quest bareback. Mr. Schultz probably thought he was a real klutz driver, jolting suddenly forward, then throttling back.

Yellow eyes caught in the headlights, then disappeared. Too short for a wolf—must have been a fox. Maybe Matt was thinking about wolves now. And if he were lost, he'd be fighting down big-time panic. Seth had never really been lost, not for more than fifteen or twenty minutes anyway, like the time when he went canoeing with his dad and mom. After they'd set up camp, he hopped in the canoe to explore. Before long, he'd circled one small island, then another, and realized he had no idea which way to head back to camp. The sky was gray, the sun absent, leaving no clue of north, west, east, or south. Panic had started at his toes and lit like a gasoline-fed bonfire. He only lived with the feeling for a few minutes before he heard his parents call his name. Hearing his name had never felt so good before. When he returned, he realized they were just calling him in for dinner. He never let them know he'd been lost. After that, he always carried a compass.

Compass! Matt didn't even have a compass, Seth realized as a cold, sick feeling enveloped him. At the last minute, Matt hadn't been able to find his own. "I've got mine," Seth had said, "so it's okay. We're hunting together."

Guilt jabbed him. He could kick himself! He shouldn't have left Matt, even if Matt *had* shot a wolf.

The four-wheeler's headlight illuminated a round

boulder, topped with a layer of new snow. At least the snowstorm hadn't hit with full force yet. Maybe the weatherman was wrong. Just drive, Seth told himself. Find him.

With Mr. Schultz's bulky body towering behind him, Seth felt as if he were three years old. Was this how Matt felt around his dad? Was that why he was always trying to prove himself?

Rumbling around another curve in the trail, the headlight caught two does, stunned motionless by the light. Seth squeezed the brake handle hard, slamming the four-wheeler to nearly a dead stop. The deer gathered their legs and, in one leap, were absorbed into white-frocked balsam.

Seth wiggled his toes; he could feel them now, warm in layers of thick wool. They were going to be fine. Then he gave the four-wheeler gas and headed farther down the trail. Past the giant pine, Seth drove his four-wheeler to the side of the trail and turned off the motor.

Mr. Schultz lifted his two-hundred-some pounds off first. Seth followed.

Stubby pulled four flashlights from a backpack and handed them out. "Okay, Seth. We're following you."

Seth gripped the long-handled flashlight, pushed the button, and swung the light back and forth until he found the narrow path leading to the beaver dam. He took a deep breath. "This way," he said, then started off, hoping and praying like crazy that the expedition wouldn't come up empty-handed.

Seth swallowed his fears. True, he'd wished Matt would have to pay a price. But not this big a price.

"Maaattt!!" Mr. Schultz called. No answer. They all shouted his name in unison. Still no answer. Mr. Schultz tried once more, and Seth strained to hear the words "Here I am!" but Matt's voice wasn't in the wind that swept through the trees.

"Okay," Mr. Schultz said, "let's keep going."

Seth walked on for maybe five minutes, clumping awkwardly in his father's boots, stumbling more than once, and stopping every few yards to call and listen. Then he hurried ahead again, pushing past scraggly branches. The woods looked completely different. He aimed his flashlight, identifying a stump here, a snowy boulder there, landmarks that helped reassure him he was still on the right path.

As they approached the beaver dam, snowflakes continued to fall, one by one, swirling in the white beam.

"Hope the storm holds off a little longer," Brett said from behind.

"We've gotta be gettin' close to your deer stand, right?" Mr. Schultz asked, worry tinting his voice. "If Matt's smart," he added almost hopefully, "he'd be waiting right there."

The deer stand. "Uh . . . we never got to my deer stand," Seth said quietly.

"What?!" Mr. Schultz sounded stunned. "Then he may have wandered . . . may not have a clue . . ."

"We'll find him," Brett said firmly. "Seth, just keep going."

At the dam, Seth stopped and turned to face Mr. Schultz and his oldest sons, their flashlight beams darting eerily into endless shadows and flecks of white. "Careful," Seth said, "I fell in here earlier. It's slippery."

Then he headed across. On the other side, he turned and directed his light on the dam. Mr. Schultz looked like Frankenstein walking a tightrope. At any other time, it would have been funny.

Chapter 11

Without warning, before Brett and Stubby finished crossing the beaver dam, wind howled down from the ridges near Mackenzie Lake, blasting sheets of white snow. Seth trudged forward, head down, trying to avoid the biting snow flying directly into his eyes. Stinging.

"What's this?" Mr. Schultz said, ripping a jacket and a down vest from a tree branch.

Seth felt weak. "We were too hot, and, well, we took off a few layers. . . ."

Mr. Schultz's face pinched with pain. "We've gotta find him. Oh God, help us find him." Then he cupped his gloves by his face. "Maaattt!" he called, his voice desperate, raw with anxiety. "Maaattt! Can you hear me?"

If Matt could hear, if he tried to answer, there was no

way they would hear him now. Pine trees groaned and dead trees cracked.

Brett and Stubby shouted, too, and Seth joined in, but the wind hurled their words into the air.

Seth trudged along the base of the ridge, picked his way carefully up the slope, slippery with new snow, and headed to the bay where he'd deserted Matt. He'd go there, to the place where they'd last been, and then what? If Matt had tried to find his way home and got lost . . . He couldn't think that far. If Matt was lost . . . A deep heaviness filled him. He hadn't been thinking clearly when he took off. He hadn't considered the consequences then. Things happen. Tragic things.

His flashlight cast a wedge shape into the woods, and Seth followed it along the faint deer trail.

"Matt!" he called, approaching the cedars where they'd stood. Matt's brothers and father joined in.

A muffled groan.

He'd heard it, a faint human sound.

Seth's light cut through darkness until it rested on a bulky form at the edge of the bay where the bucks had fought. For a fleeting second, Seth wondered if Matt had somehow been attacked by the injured wolf. But the form wasn't Matt; it was only a boulder.

"Hey," came Matt's groggy voice from another direction.

Where was he? Seth swung his light toward the low sweeping branches of a balsam. He hurried, knelt on the snow, and peered closer. Under the branches, on a patch of brown needles, Matt was on the ground curled up like a baby.

"Here he is!" Seth yelled.

Matt slowly lifted to his hands and knees, crawled toward the circle of light, then flopped on his back at their feet, light shining into his blinking eyes. A dried leaf clung to his hair, which snuck out from under his orange cap, and his skin was bluish gray.

"I thought I could get back," Matt said, his words slow and thick, "but I made a loop. To here. Stayed put. Knew you'd come, eventually. Got so tired . . ."

Seth, flooded with relief, exhaled hard.

Mr. Schultz hoisted Matt to his feet, one hand under his arm. "Thank God we found you."

Matt's legs wobbled, and he tottered.

"Better carry you," Mr. Schultz said. "You must have hypothermia."

"No, I'm . . . ," Matt protested, but his father swept him off the ground.

"Seth," he said, "lead us back."

Seth set off quickly. Hypothermia wasn't something to take lightly. A person could die from getting too cold. If he had kept his head about him, this would never have happened.

As Mr. Schultz crossed the dam, he said, "Matt, good thing you didn't beef up too much this year."

"My coach wishes . . . ," Matt said, but he didn't finish his sentence.

His coach wishes he weighed ten to twelve more pounds, Seth could have finished for him. Seth knew Matt inside out. Or he had thought he did, until today.

Snow and wind stung Seth's cheeks. His toes and fingers were beginning to feel stiff, almost disconnected from the rest of his body. If he was getting chilled, Matt had to be numb after spending hours and hours in the woods. Seth walked faster.

At the four-wheelers, snow layered the seats. Seth hopped on, started one four-wheeler, and waited in a white cloud of exhaust. Instead of using the trailer, Brett and Stubby squeezed Matt between them. Mr.

Schultz climbed on behind Seth, and they started off.

Crawling back to the Schultzes' house, Seth wiped at the snow gathering on his lashes, freezing the corners of his eyelids together. He could barely see! The trail disappeared to a thin, vague opening through speckled white. Snow swirled, whipped his face raw, and he wished he had a windshield.

The second early storm of the season, a whiteout. Every year, somewhere in Minnesota, someone died during a blizzard, trying to outsmart it. Someone would lose control of their car and get stuck in a snowbank, leave their vehicle, and then try to walk for help. They'd lose their way in the blowing snow, lose their way in the endless white. When the snowstorm stopped, and the sun shone again and the snowplows scraped the roads clean, another frozen body would be found, usually only yards from the vehicle.

Seth thought of that now. And he knew, as he drove down the trail, that Brett and Stubby and Mr. Schultz knew it, too—were thinking about what might have happened if they hadn't found Matt in time.

He hunkered himself down, peering over the handlebars, squinting to see the trail. Slowly, he motored back, out of the woods, down Matt's driveway through deepening snow, and over to the Schultzes' barn, whose yellow floodlight glowed like a lighthouse in swirling fog.

Mr. Schultz hopped off the four-wheeler, rolled open the metal door, and waved his sons and Seth inside. Seth throttled forward, out of the wind, then cut the motor.

"Hello there," came a familiar voice.

Seth jumped, looking around.

"Over here. Ray Kruppa." Opposite the snowmobiles, he dropped the plastic sheet over the dead calf and strode toward them. His brown eyes were somber, yet warm as a low-burning fire.

"Seth," he said, nodding. Seth had known Ray Kruppa for years through his father's work. Kruppa held out his hand to Mr. Schultz. "I know it's late, but when I heard the weather report, I hustled over to investigate the field site. I had to brush away snow, but your wife told me where to look."

Mr. Schultz quickly shook the offered hand, then pointed over his shoulder. "Gotta get my son inside. Might have hypothermia."

Seth's throat grew hot.

Ray Kruppa glanced beyond Mr. Schultz at Matt, who

stood between his brothers. Seth watched from a distance, seated on the four-wheeler. He wanted to shout, "I'm sorry! I shouldn't have left him out there!" He bit down on the fleshy inside of his lip. His eyes burned. He wasn't going to let himself cry, not here. And it didn't help that Mr. Schultz was acting nice. Anger might be easier than this. Nobody was saying it out loud but it was more than obvious—he'd screwed up.

"Mind if I use your phone?" Kruppa asked. "I have to call the vet about this calf, get her to come out first thing."

"No problem," Mr. Schultz said, heaving wide the door to the swirling white. "There's one in the barn here, but you might as well come in the house."

"Let's get some hot chocolate," Brett said, his arm under Matt's shoulder.

"Yeah," Stubby added, "and to mine, I'm adding a stiff shot of brandy."

Seth followed the Schultzes and Ray Kruppa across the yard, his head tucked down, shoulders hunched to keep the wind from creeping down his neck.

Chapter 12

Blue-and-orange flames danced around birch logs in the glass-doored woodstove. Stretched out in his sleeping bag, Seth cupped his chin in his hands, elbows propped on his pillow, and watched the fire. Mrs. Schultz insisted that Kruppa spend the night, due to the "terrible weather," and take Matt's room. With all the other lights off, the fire cast a glow in the family room, illuminating the glass eyes of the bear and deer. Seth was glad Mr. Schultz hadn't put up a stuffed wolf from his earlier hunting years.

Bubbles of sap formed on the logs, then dripped, sputtering into red dusty coals.

The house was quiet. Seth couldn't sleep. Too many thoughts clammered in his head.

Matt groaned, wiggled like a caterpillar in its cocoon,

then settled into silence again.

"Matt?" Seth asked. "You awake?"

No answer.

Seth watched the flames, the way they curled up at the far wall of the woodstove. Matt was going to be okay. They'd shuffled him inside the house, stripped him down to his red boxers, wrapped him in blankets, and set him by the fire. While he shook uncontrollably, they spooned him noodle soup and hot chocolate, and when he finished that, Brett made up a platter of nachos smothered with meat, black olives, green peppers, and cheese. The hot sauce packed a punch, producing tiny droplets of sweat on Seth's brow. It had to help Matt warm up, too, because by the time he was done eating, he was kicking off blankets, complaining of burning up. Who wouldn't, wrapped in five blankets?

But it was finding him in the woods, curled in a ball, that Seth couldn't shake. Everything was fine, Matt was okay. But inside, Seth felt rotten. What kind of a friend was he? If Matt had died, it would have been his fault. Matt was alive, but everything *wasn't* okay. The rip in their friendship felt like a deep flesh wound.

Matt twisted in his bag, flipping himself over to face

Seth. His eyes fluttered, opened halfway, then he turned away. Heck, maybe he wasn't even awake, Seth told himself, or he would have said something.

Fact was, they hadn't said a word to each other since Matt was found. Not one word.

Seth dropped his head on the pillow, filled his lungs with a deep breath, and closed his eyes. So what if they weren't friends anymore? He had other friends, just no one he knew so well.

Come morning, he was heading home. Plain and simple.

"Why, Seth, of course you're staying for breakfast!" Mrs. Schultz said, waving him to the dining room table. "Your animals can wait for you to finish my famous blueberry pancakes, can't they?"

Seth paused in the entry, glanced at the clock above the Schultzes' yellow stove 7:20—and reluctantly eased his arm out of his jacket. He had to get out of there. "Okay," he said, his voice flat, "but I have to get going soon."

Smells of sausage and coffee filled the sunny house.

Kruppa lifted a tall glass of orange juice to his lips.

"Hey, Seth, I'd like to see that moose calf after breakfast, before the vet gets here. Last time I saw it, it looked 'bout dead."

"Sure," Seth said, and sat in the only available chair, right next to Matt. He wished Matt had slept late, but despite his ordeal, Matt was up with the birds, as usual.

Squinting, Seth looked out the window. A grumbling snowplow pushed its wide blade along the road. Drifts, in some places five feet high, sculpted the Schultzes' yard. The barn-style bird feeder wore a foot of snow. Both driveways were already plowed; Mr. Schultz must have gotten up hours earlier. Under the early rays of winter light, snow sparkled, and usually Seth would have felt a tingle of excitement at the mounds of new snow.

Mr. Schultz bowed his head and everyone followed, everyone except Seth. "Bless us, Oh Lord, for these Thy gifts . . ."

Today, he couldn't join in. He watched the bowed heads, listened to the words. What about the "gifts" of nature, he wanted to say? What about the wolf Matt shot, isn't that a gift worth blessing? And what about himself? He wasn't sure he deserved God's blessing, not now.

Mrs. Schultz added another stack of steaming

pancakes to the plate in the center of the table. "Ray, I want you to know that these berries are from the rocky ridge along the north edge of our property. A bumper crop last summer."

North edge. Seth didn't have to see Matt to read his mind. That's where they'd found Star.

"Mmm," Kruppa responded. "Great breakfast."

"Thanks," she said. She placed a hand on the back of Matt's head. "You feeling better this morning, honey?"

Matt nodded, his mouth full.

"That's good," she said, and sat down. "Gave us quite a scare last night."

Seth glanced at Kruppa, then sideways at Matt, whose face was stony. Getting stuck in the woods, he wanted to say, maybe brought you an armload of sympathy, but it still doesn't erase what you did. *What I did.*

"You know, I'm noticing," Mrs. Schultz continued, carefully choosing her words, "that you boys haven't said as much as a word to each other since last night."

Seth stared at his plate, at the way the blueberries stained the pancake.

"Am I right?" she pressed.

He always spread his pancakes out in a wide circle,

then ate them one at a time. Matt, on the other hand, stacked his pancakes, then cut them like a pie. When they were younger, they'd argued about which way was best.

"Angel," Mr. Schultz said. "They're old enough to figure out their differences on their own." As if to change the subject, he added, "Well, let's hope Brett and Stubby get their deer today, huh?"

Seth puffed a stream of air from his nostrils. Figure out our differences? Don't bet on it, he wanted to say. Don't bet on it.

Chapter 13

Snow had drifted into a cresting wave against the Jacobsons' barn door. Pushing the silver snow scoop into the drift, Seth slowly cleared a path. Kruppa used a smaller shovel and cleared the steps to the house's back door.

A quiet had settled over everything, as though nature was resting now that the storm had passed. Black-capped chickadees darted in and out of the bird feeder, from which Seth had brushed away snow.

"I'm done," Seth called over his shoulder.

Kruppa stuck his shovel in a snowbank. "Okay."

Seth stepped in and, before his eyes could adjust, heard a clatter of hooves. Something was amiss. He stopped, Kruppa right behind him. "Just a second," he said. "Better close the door."

Quest snorted from his stall. The air was ripe with manure. At the far end of the barn, in the walkway, the calf was pacing.

"Uh-oh," Seth said. "It's out of its stall. Now what?"

"You got a halter or a lead rope on it?" Kruppa said, stepping alongside Seth.

"Nope. Wish I had." Seth felt himself buckle inside. How was he supposed to lead Fudge back into the stall?

"How do you think it got out?"

"I must have forgotten to bolt the stall door." Seth couldn't just let it wander around, or he wouldn't be able to clean the stalls or anything. "I touched the calf the other day. Think I should just go up to it and—?"

"No," Kruppa said firmly, stroking the short curly hairs of his beard. "No, I don't think so, not if it's ever going to return to the wild. You don't want it to bond with you, to get tame. Otherwise, it will be too trusting of people, easy prey during moose-hunting season. It needs its wildness."

The calf stood still, its head turned toward them, watching. A thickness grew in Seth's throat, a swell of mixed feelings. He'd let himself believe that touching the calf, becoming friends with it, was a good thing.

"He's thin, but y'know, Seth, he looks pretty healthy to me," Kruppa said. "The sooner he gets back outside, the better, otherwise he won't have the coat he needs." He paused. "Any reason you shouldn't let him go?"

Seth swallowed. Any reason? That he wanted him for a pet, to keep him? What kind of a reason was that? He struggled for other reasons. "Well, he scraped against a rusty nail," Seth said. "Probably should get a tetanus shot."

"Melanie could help you out there."

"Melanie?"

"The vet."

"Oh yeah." Seth took three steps to Quest, ran the flat of his hand against the horse's face, his fingers tracing the fine cheekbones. He kept a lookout for the calf. "Then there's the problem of letting it go with so many wolves around."

"That's reality, Seth," Kruppa said matter-of-factly, as if he didn't care what happened.

Seth glared at him. "Reality? Is that all you can say?" He'd seen enough kill sites. "Fudge isn't just another moose! I saved him!"

Kruppa moved to the hay bales, sat down, his gaze resting on the moose calf, who stared cowlike from the

91

shadows outside its box stall. Kruppa's mouth worked, but he didn't say a word, as if he were leaving the decision in the air.

And Seth left it there, suspended like a hot-air balloon. "Can you wait here?" he asked. "I'm gonna run in and get some more fruit and vegetables. It ate some earlier, so I'm thinking, if I bring out another bucketful, place it in the stall, and get the door to stay wide open, maybe it'll just go back in on its own." He felt himself talking fast, as if racing against time.

"Sure," Kruppa said. "You do what you need to do."

Outside, a gunshot sounded to the east. *Ka-blam-blam-blam*. Hunting season. He'd almost forgotten. Another good reason to keep the moose calf inside, at least for two more weeks.

He stepped in the back door, nearly tripping on Midnight, who wove in and out of his legs, purring like rain on a metal roof. The smells of his own home, his mother's vanilla candle on the table, of everything in it, made him suddenly homesick. When were his parents—and little Lizzy—coming home?

He pushed the play button on the answering machine.

"This is for Seth," came the familiar nasal voice. "Hi, Seth. This is Bart Bishop, you know, from the last home-school meeting at the park. Anyway, maybe you want to come over sometime. Call me if you want to do something." He left a number, but Seth wasn't anxious to return the call. Maybe things were over with Matt, but he didn't need a friend that badly, not yet anyway.

Beep. "Seth, you know who this is"—it was his mother—"but do you know this voice?" A soft crying came over the machine. Seth thought he'd hate to hear crying, but right now, it sounded better than anything in the world. "If you guessed Lizzy, you're right. She's just beautiful, Seth, and it brings back memories of when you were little. I miss you, but I'll see you soon. We're waiting for the doctor's visit, and then we'll be discharged. Um, it's before eight. Should be there around lunchtime."

Seth glanced at the clock. He'd missed their call by only a half hour. Quickly, he fed Midnight, dashed food on the top of his aquarium for his angelfish, then cut up the remaining lettuce, cucumber, apple, and oranges for Fudge. He'd cleaned out the fridge, and yet the ice-cream bucket was less than half full. Even if the moose calf loved fresh food, Seth's parents could never afford the grocery bill. And the pellet food was going fast. Fudge needed large quantities of cheaper food, the kind found only in the woods, he thought as he hustled back to the barn.

"Nice work," Kruppa said, after Seth lured the moose calf back into its stall and double checked the bolt.

Scrrrrch, Scrrrrch. Seth turned. "Quest is going to go crazy! Two weeks of hunting season. He'll chew his stall apart! I've gotta come up with a way to let him stretch out."

"Orange tape," Kruppa said. "Got any?"

On a dusty shelf, Seth found a roll of orange plastic tape his father had used to mark dead birch trees on the edge of the property. Trees slated for cutting. Quest put his head over his stall and nibbled at the roll of tape.

"I've seen others use it," Kruppa said. "They tie the strips to the mane, tail, halter, whatever."

"With this," Seth said to Quest, "you can go outside, at least close to the barn."

Soon Seth was leading Quest out of his stall. Quest's hooves clomped an anxious staccato beat. Seth opened the pasture door wide and unclipped the lead.

"Stretch out," he said, motioning toward the corral, a

fenced area inside the wider pasture.

Quest tossed his mane, gathered his legs beneath him, and, decorated in dancing strips of orange, cantered around the corral in a wide circle. He stopped and kicked out his back legs.

Seth smiled.

Kruppa was at his side. "That'll work," he said.

As Quest lay down to roll, Seth walked from post to post, stringing orange tape around the corral's perimeter. A hunter would have to be blind to miss that.

When they stepped back in the barn, the moose calf was reaching for cedar leaves piled on the straw, pulling them toward itself across the floor.

"If I let *you* outside," Seth said, avoiding Kruppa's eyes, "I may not get you back in again."

"Now let's head back to the Schultzes'," Kruppa said. "I want to make a quick trek into the woods before the vet gets here or I get another call."

"Nah," Seth replied, not wanting to be around Matt any more than he had to, "you go on. I'm fine here."

"Come on," Kruppa said, turning and waving Seth to join him. "I've got an idea you might want to join me."

Why couldn't he just say no? Seth hesitated, then

followed Kruppa into the blinding sunlight. As they walked down the plowed driveway, he told Kruppa about the deer kill they'd found, the howling he'd heard lately, and finding Star in the field.

"Wolf numbers are way up," Kruppa said, "and that's great. Up until 1967, they were trapped and hunted almost to extinction. They're returning to Wisconsin and Michigan, too, but it takes time. Now if we can just get people to stop seeing wolves as their enemy."

Seth told Kruppa about the conversation he'd heard at the hospital.

"Oh yeah," said Kruppa as they crossed the road to Matt's house. "That kind of thinking is tough to change. You can only do it one slow step at a time."

At the Schultzes' doorstep, Seth ran his gloved finger through the white mound of snow along the railing. He didn't mind Kruppa, but he really couldn't handle this. He turned away, started down the steps.

"Seth, stick around," Kruppa said, knocking.

"Door's open!" Mr. Schultz answered from inside.

Seth found himself walking back up the entry steps and stepping reluctantly inside the Schultzes' house. He didn't want to face Matt.

Chapter 14

Mr. and Mrs. Schultz were doing the dishes. The aroma of coffee filled the air.

Kruppa stood in the entry. "I've got an idea Matt and Seth just might be interested in," he said.

"Let's hear," said Mr. Schultz, waving Kruppa forward. "Matt, come here."

Matt appeared from the living room but stood at a distance, holding up the wall with his shoulder.

"Yesterday afternoon," Kruppa explained, "my receiver showed that one of the wolves in Pack Thirty-six was stationary, not moving. And when I checked again this morning, Big Gray still hadn't moved."

"Big Gray?" Matt asked with a snort. "You actually *named* a wolf?"

"Well, that's the name I gave him," Kruppa explained.

"It fits—he's big and mostly gray."

He scanned the faces in the room. "Looks like its close by, so I'm going to take a quick trek and see what I can find out. Who knows, he might need to be freed from a trap." He looked back toward Seth. "Anyway, as a kind of learning opportunity, I thought the boys here might want to join me."

Mr. Schultz curved his lower lip, shrugged his shoulders. "I don't see why not."

"But . . . ," Matt said, glancing at Seth. His brown eyes were sharp, warning. *Don't say a word.* "I better help with the cows."

"We can handle chores this morning, Matt," said Mrs. Schultz. "You go ahead. Might do you and Seth some good."

"Besides, you can't hunt till we're free to go," said Mr. Schultz. He nodded at Kruppa. "Which will be just as soon as we're assured our money for that calf."

Before they left, fully dressed in orange for protection from other hunters, Kruppa stopped by his pickup truck and pulled out two rectangular black boxes. "Receivers," he said, handing one to each of the boys. Then he handed them antenna grids. "Yagi antennas," he explained. "Each collared wolf has its own transmitter signal. You'll be able to help locate Big Gray–Number 273."

Seth opened the receiver case and studied the knobs and monitor needle.

Matt held his receiver but was staring past Kruppa, toward his snowy field.

"Well," Kruppa said enthusiastically, "let's head out. Our destination point," he said, checking his compass and rumpled map like a Boy Scout leader, "will be the northwest edge of Mackenzie Lake." He looked up. "You guys know a quick way to get there?"

"Yeah," Matt volunteered, nodding toward his barn. "Snowmobiles."

Within minutes, they were on two Arctic Cats. Matt led the way, with Seth and Kruppa following, riding double. The snowmobiles glided through waves of deep fluff, flying along the wide trail. At the towering pine, they stopped and hopped off, tracking equipment in hand.

Seth broke trail through knee-deep snow. He turned at a familiar V-shaped tree, a dip in the creamy landscape, a hole-riddled stump, until he came to the beaver dam, sweat forming under his jacket. Sun glinted off the snow into his eyes. He remembered his own words: "I swear, if you stand up, I'm gonna hit you!" He'd never been angrier with Matt, at what he'd done. ". . . You find your own stupid way home!" But he'd never done something so careless before. And though he wanted to point a finger at Matt, the finger kept pointing back to himself.

He stopped. A soft trickling sounded from the snow-covered creek, water running beneath ice.

Kruppa planted his feet. "By air, a receiver can pick up the signal from up to five miles, but on the ground it's only a quarter mile, at most." He glanced over his shoulder. "Hey, Matt. Still with us?"

"Yeah," Matt said, his voice low.

"I think your bout with the cold knocked some life out of you, eh?" Kruppa asked.

Matt walked up closer, stopped a few feet off. "Maybe."

Seth looked away, pretending to study the beaver dam. "Slipped here yesterday," he said, "so be careful."

"Oh? You were out here, Seth?"

Matt leveled his brown eyes on Seth.

"Uh, yeah . . . guess you could say we came by here."

Kruppa nodded. "Hunting?"

"Uh-huh."

"See any action?" Kruppa asked.

Seth glanced at Matt, then shook his head. He couldn't meet Kruppa's eyes. "No, not really."

"Well," Kruppa said, pausing. "Why don't I lead from here on out, if that's okay with you."

"Fine," Seth answered, letting Kruppa cross the dam first, arms out for balance.

Matt elbowed Seth hard, knocking the air from his chest, then started after Kruppa across the dam.

"Watch it!" Seth said under his breath.

"Don't worry," Kruppa replied, nearing the dam's length. "I'm being careful."

A rush of embarrassment warmed Seth's face. Matt. That jerk.

They pushed on through thick cedar, a low area further north of Mackenzie Lake where Seth had never explored. Kruppa stopped. "Here," he said. "Let's set our receivers." He showed each of them how to set their dials to 273 and point their Yagi antennas. Seth swung the antenna slowly back and forth in front of him while Kruppa led Matt twenty or so yards to the left.

"Okay," Kruppa called, "hold your positions." Then, with a compass reading and two intersecting coordinates, Kruppa determined the wolf's position and led the rest of the way. "Getting closer," he said time and again.

Seth and Matt followed, avoiding glances.

At the base of a west-facing slope dotted with white pine, Kruppa stopped and pointed to one old tree, jutting like an *L* out of the hill.

Just beneath the tree's trunk, a hole the size of a basketball gaped in the snow. "Yup," he whispered. "I think that's where he's denned up. At least we didn't find him in a snare or trap. But there's no movement. Either his collar fell off, or . . ."

Kruppa hiked closer, examining the snow. Seth looked, too, but didn't notice any fresh tracks. If there was a wolf in the den, he went in yesterday before the snow fell. What if a whole pack was in there? He shivered, then told himself to calm down. Get a grip.

"Okay, guys," Kruppa said. "I'm gonna try to crawl in. You hang back."

"You're what!? W-what if it's alive?" Seth whispered. "Won't it attack?"

Kruppa shook his head. "At this point, I doubt it's

alive, but the answer is no. Wolf hunters used to enter dens, sometimes with the alpha female inside. They'd shoot the pups and she never attacked. Then, unfortunately, they'd shoot her, too."

"Probably shot 'em," Matt said flatly, "because they stole livestock."

"Y'know, Matt, sometimes I have to do that," Kruppa said, digging a flashlight from his backpack, "trap and shoot a wolf that has gone after livestock. *Worst* part of what I do."

Matt shuffled uneasily back and forth, nearly bouncing, the way he did before the start of a football game. Seth watched him, stomach churning.

Next to the den's entrance, Kruppa got down on his knees, then began pulling away at rocks until the hole widened.

Boom! boom! came the echoes of a distant gun. Maybe Brett or Stubby got a deer.

A breeze swept overhead, sending down a shower of white clumps. Branches swayed, and a mound of snow softly plopped on Seth's shoulder.

Kruppa slid his arms, then his chest, inside, his legs sticking out from the hole.

103

Matt turned to Seth and mouthed, "You better not say a word."

"Believe me," Seth whispered, "I'm tempted!" But deep down, he didn't think he could, couldn't actually turn his friend in, even if their friendship was demolished.

"Some friend you were, leaving me out there," Matt said. "I could have died!"

"Well, you didn't. And at least I didn't break the law!"

"Oh, don't give me that! You're so out of touch with reality. Think you know everything. Well, you don't!"

Seth squared his shoulders. He didn't have to take this.

"At least I think with my brains," he said, glaring, "not with my butt."

Matt lunged, hitting Seth with full force. He grabbed Seth around the waist, tackled him into the snow, and slammed the air out of his lungs.

"Oof!"

Seth crumpled and felt himself plow backward against a bush, slide downward—*bump, slam, crunch*—over rocks beneath the snow. He grabbed for a hold on a passing bush, on Matt, anything to slow his fall. But Matt was clamped on like iron, plowing him inch by inch to the bottom of the slope. Snow iced down his neck and up his wrists.

Finally, Seth stopped, his head jammed into a rock.

"Back off!" he shouted, his arms exploding, forcing Matt away.

Matt collapsed backward in the snow, facing the sky. "That felt good!" His chest rose and fell.

Seth scooped two handfuls of snow, smashed them into Matt's face, then jumped to his feet. "How 'bout that? Does that feel good?"

"You little . . ." Matt was on his knees, slamming into Seth's legs again, bringing him down with a thud.

"Hey!" yelled Kruppa. "You two!"

Matt stopped, pulling back. Seth rose to his feet and looked up the hill.

At the top, Kruppa was standing outside the den, the still form of a gray wolf at his feet. The heather gray wolf they'd watched. The animal that had disappeared into the woods—shot. Seth felt sick. He'd sensed it might come to this. Sadness and anger rose up in him, and he turned away.

Chapter 15

Kruppa rummaged in his backpack, whipped out a camera, and snapped pictures of the wolf, then pulled out a clipboard and pen. "Gut-shot," he said, his voice somber, filling in a form. "Someone shot it, then it came back here . . . to an abandoned den. Body's still a touch warm. Lost lots of blood, so it couldn't have been shot too long ago, yesterday at most. Made it here, obviously, before the snow came." He looked up, his eyes stormy. "I see too many like this. Unless someone steps forward and confesses," he said, voice controlled, "we'll never know who did it. . . ."

Matt hung back, his gaze fixed on the wolf.

Seth swallowed. Did Kruppa know? Of course not. How could he? Seth felt the knowledge of Matt's secret smoldering in his mind, like a fire in a peat bog, quietly burning beneath the surface. He hated this. He wanted to say something, to shout it out, but he couldn't, wouldn't turn in Matt.

Calling loudly, a pileated woodpecker flew overhead. Seth watched it land on a dead tree riddled with holes. *Dat-dat-dat-dat!* It pounded with its beak, flecks of wood flying, its red and black foot-long body bobbing.

Seth trudged closer to the wolf, the *shh-shh* of his hunting pants rubbing together as he moved. He brushed melting snow from his face, then squatted next to the wolf's large head and long snout. Its black lip was lifted slightly, revealing sharp teeth. He pulled off his glove and touched the white and gray long hairs, the ruff, a regal fur collar, around its face. He tried to avoid, but couldn't help seeing, the dark blood matted on the animal's sides.

"Think it had a family?" Matt asked, his voice startling Seth. What did he care?

"Used to be part of a pack," Kruppa replied. "He's a three-year-old male that might have been trying to prove himself. I have the feeling he was recently booted out by the alpha male and female. The pack only allows for one breeding pair, and so occasionally, a wolf like Big Gray here will move on, traveling alone, joining another pack, or following his own pack from a distance. They're highly intelligent animals, with their own rules of order." Kruppa looked somewhere beyond the boys. "What a waste," he said. "I just don't understand it."

Seth glanced at Matt, whose eyes were glistening, fixed on the motionless form. Kruppa attached a rope to the wolf's collar and pulled it through the snow. The boys walked behind in silence. When they finally reached the trail, Kruppa asked Matt, "Mind if I strap Big Gray behind you?"

Matt stared straight ahead, waiting, then started his snowmobile and slowly headed home.

When they returned to the Schultzes', a white van marked NORTHWOODS ANIMAL HOSPITAL was parked under the leafless willow between Stubby's red pickup and Kruppa's truck.

"Looks like she beat us," Kruppa said. He carefully placed the wolf's stiff body into the back of his pickup. With a wrench, he loosened the bolts of the radio collar, removed it, then shut the tailgate. "Maybe that wasn't such a great experience for you two after all," he said, looking out at the sky, wispy with pale clouds. "Would have been better had we been able to free an animal from a trap, do something good, eh?" Kruppa sighed. "A shot wolf. Means I'll have to bring in a federal agent now."

Matt's lips parted as if he were going to say something, but nothing came out.

Then Kruppa led the were inside the metal barn, where Mr. and Mrs. Schultz stood beside Star's body. The vet rose from her squatting position.

"Ray," she said, a quick smile crossing her face like sunshine. "Glad you're here." Seth quickly put it together. He wasn't stupid. There was something between these two.

"It died of blackleg," she said. "Your suspicions were right. You can feel the bubbles under its coat."

"But we were there!" Matt blurted. "We saw the wolf tracks, the blood. What do you mean, 'blackleg'?"

Kruppa looked at Matt, as if studying his sudden outburst.

"Well, the wolves obviously fed on it after it died," said the vet, "but from what I can see . . ."

"The blood," Kruppa interjected, "for one thing, was a darker blue color and blotted, not spread out on the snow."

"Right," said the vet. "Wolf predation wasn't the

cause of death. It died of natural causes."

"So what's blackleg?" Seth asked.

Matt glanced at him, muttered under his breath, "As if you care."

Seth pretended he didn't hear and squared his shoulders.

"Well," the vet explained, brushing bangs off her forehead with the back of her rubber-gloved hand, fingers tipped reddish brown. "It's a disease that strikes suddenly in the fall. One moment, you have a healthy cow—or calf—and the next thing you know, it's down. The bacteria cause a swelling and blackening of infected muscle tissue. Comes on with no warning." She glanced over her shoulder at the corralled cows. "And the real problem is that it can rapidly spread to the rest of the herd. Finding that calf and calling in help immediately was the best thing that could have happened."

"Oh, thanks," Matt said sarcastically. "That makes me feel a whole lot better about losing my calf."

"What I mean is," the vet continued, "the wolves helped alert us to the real problem sooner. Now, the next step is to vaccinate the whole herd. Immediately, with your okay," she said, nodding at Mr. and Mrs. Schultz.

Mrs. Schultz spoke up. "I don't think we have much choice, do we?"

"Not really," replied the vet. "If we do it now, the vaccine will still take five days to take effect." She headed toward the door. "I have supplies in my van. Be right back."

"Well, I'll be . . . ," Mr. Schultz said, arms crossed. "Blackleg. Now you don't have to go kill a wolf, Ray."

No, someone's already done that job, Seth thought.

Kruppa nodded, but something seemed to be rolling around in his mind, his gaze falling somewhere beyond Mr. Schultz.

"But," Matt said, turning to Kruppa, almost pleading, "wolves trespassed, came right into our pasture!"

Kruppa nodded again.

"So who's to say they won't come back?" Matt continued.

Kruppa scratched at his beard, scanned the whole Schultz family. "You mentioned before that this calf's mother died of pneumonia. . . ."

"Yeah," said Mr. Schultz. "What's your point?"

"To be direct," Kruppa said, rubbing the beard hairs along his jawline, "where did you dispose of the body?"

111

"Dragged it out beyond the north fence line, like always," Mr. Schultz volunteered.

"Perhaps that's part of the problem," said Kruppa. "Wolves probably fed off the carcass, then returned, looking for more. This time, make sure that calf's body is hauled away, and you'll minimize the risk of having wolves return."

"And if they do?" asked Mr. Schultz, sweeping his arm to the north. "I mean, it's miles of woods out there. There must be some blasted way to keep the herd safe."

"You might try dogs—Great Pyrenees—or a llama or two," suggested Kruppa.

"Llamas?" Mr. Schultz snorted. "A joke, right?"

Kruppa shook his head. "No joke. I've seen a big dog try to go after a calf. The llama spotted it from far away, then walked straight for it. The dog bolted, tail between its legs. Anyway, they'll scare wolves off, too. But they spit," Kruppa added, "green stuff. So if you get one, stay alert."

Matt stood by Star's form, shoulders hunched. Seth started to feel sorry for him, but then turned silently away and started toward the door.

He stopped when the vet stepped back into the barn.

"Ray?" she asked, passing him with a black supply case. "That wolf in your truck. What happened?"

"Shot," he said. "Senselessly. Seth was telling me about some hunters he overheard, and maybe there's something there. . . . But if it was a minor," Kruppa continued, "someone younger, you understand, who thought it had killed a favorite calf from their herd. . . ."

"Hey, now," Mr. Schultz said, pressing both palms forward. "If you're suggesting that Matt did anything . . ." His bulky frame seemed to puff up.

Seth's feet were planted in the dirt floor.

Mr. Schultz took two steps closer to Kruppa. "My son is a quarterback, a fine athlete, and there's no way he'd go breaking the law, like you seem to be suggesting. Matt," he said, his voice controlled, "you set him straight here."

Matt, chin quivering, spun toward his dad. "But I really thought it had killed Star," he said in a rush, "and I was so mad!" He choked out the words. "Then all of sudden, Seth and I, we're out hunting, and there it was . . . and before I knew what I was doing . . ." He paused, lowered his head.

Mr. Schultz froze; only his eyes moved, looking to his

113

wife. Mrs. Schultz removed her hand from her jacket pocket and touched her fingers to her lips.

"Wait a second," Mr. Schultz said. "He doesn't know what he's talking about here."

"No," Matt volunteered. "I knew what I was doing. I shot it."

"You what?!" Mr. Schultz boomed.

Matt didn't answer, didn't look up. His voice came like a whisper. "You always said you hated wolves. I thought . . ."

Mr. Schultz heavily shook his head. "Oh, I talk tough," he said, "but I never really meant . . ."

Mrs. Schultz stepped closer to her husband, whispered in his ear, then nodded at him.

"Sometimes I say a lot of things I don't really mean," Mr. Schultz said. He gnawed at his lower lip.

Seth felt like he shouldn't be there. It had turned into a family thing. He walked over to the four-wheelers, ran his hand along one of the handles. He couldn't believe it. Matt had actually confessed.

"What does this mean for Matt?" Mrs. Schultz asked quietly.

Matt's shoulders drooped. His head hung low.

Seth knew. Jail time. Maybe thousands of dollars in fines.

Kruppa took a deep breath. "In this case, because he's young, a juvenile, and because he reacted to what he thought was predation, I'll probably talk to the federal agent and county prosecutor. Maybe suggest a different arrangement." He paused, working his finger across his beard. "Depending on his plea, of course, but possibly community service hours or working with me from time to time, helping follow the wolves from the air."

Seth watched Matt, who stood frozen, as if he'd stopped breathing.

"You know," Kruppa continued, "follow the pack, see where they travel, what their habits are . . . and understand them better."

What? Seth couldn't believe what he was hearing. Kruppa was actually going to consider letting Matt-the-jerk work with him—study the wolves—as a form of punishment? What kind of punishment was that? Matt was the last person who deserved that opportunity. A chance of a lifetime. It wasn't fair. Not at all.

An awkward silence followed until Matt broke it. He looked beyond Kruppa and met Seth's eyes. "Um . . ." He cleared his throat. "If I do that stuff, do you think Seth could come, too?" he asked, his voice raspy but sincere. "He loves wolves."

Seth felt all eyes suddenly on him. He lowered his chin and swallowed around the tightness in his throat, trying to make sense of the events of the last few days. Not only had Matt confessed, but in his own way he'd just reached out, forgiving him. Seth was stunned. For the first time he could remember, Matt hadn't tried to get the upper hand, hadn't tried to stay a notch above.

And Seth didn't know what to do with that.

Chapter 16

The barn phone rang and Mr. Schultz snatched it from the wall. "Yup," he said, nodding at Seth, "he's here. I'll send him right home."

Without a word, Seth raced out the sliding door, down the driveway, and across the road to his own house. Tire tracks rutted the snow and disappeared into the closed garage. Seth ran around to the back door, then caught his breath, slowed himself down. A baby, he thought, might need some quiet.

He stepped in, the noon sun falling on a bouquet of roses on the kitchen table. "I'm home," he called.

That afternoon, Seth learned that his sister's toes and fingers were tinier than he could've imagined, with perfect little fingernails and toenails. On the back of Lizzy's neck was a small red birthmark, "an angel kiss," his mother said. In front of the fireplace, bundled in a white flannel blanket, Lizzy rested in Seth's arms, his parents' voices filtering from the kitchen.

He lightly touched the fine wisps of hair on her head, her rosy red skin. Smelling of baby powder, she gripped his finger tightly, opened and closed her dark eyes, then drifted to sleep.

While his mother napped on the couch, Seth held Lizzy, until she woke, that is, with a piercing cry.

Mom lifted her head. "My turn," she said.

Over the following two weeks, Seth learned to change diapers, give Lizzy an evening bottle, and wrap her snugly in a blanket. To his surprise, it wasn't that bad. Along with his studies, he took care of the moose calf. While Quest was outdoors, Seth kept the barn doors open wide, so Fudge's coat wouldn't grow too thin. Twice, Seth got out with his dad to hunt, but he didn't see a thing. And more than once, he thought of calling Matt, but never knew what he'd say.

The day after hunting season ended, when the grand-father clock gonged four times and the sun slanted across the living room floor, Seth finally picked up the phone. He dialed the number he'd known by heart for years.

"Want to come over for a few minutes?"

"Why?" Matt said, hesitantly. "To talk to your dad?"

"No," Seth said, fingers twisting the phone cord. "I haven't said a word to him about anything. I figure that's between you and Kruppa."

"What then?"

"Just come. You'll see."

Seth waited at Fudge's stall, feet perched on a stall board. Fudge was pacing, snorting, nibbling at branches of dried cedar in the hay bin, then leaving it.

The wooden barn door creaked open, and Matt stepped in, his gait less springy than usual. "Hi," he said, a football grasped between his hands.

"Hi."

Matt walked past Quest's stall, which Seth had just mucked out and refloored with shining gold straw, and approached the moose.

"So," Matt asked. "What's up?"

"You and your dad okay?" Seth asked, watching the moose calf rub against the wall.

"Yeah. Actually, we had a good talk." Matt snapped and unsnapped the bottom of his letter jacket. "Anyway, I still don't know what I think about wolves,

119

but I screwed up—big time." He paused, hands still. "First time I saw that wolf, all I could think of was Star—and I hated it. Later, when I saw it close up— dead—I couldn't believe I'd actually killed it. I don't feel very good about it."

Neither spoke.

Seth knew what it felt like to waste an animal. When he'd killed the wild rabbit, it felt good for a moment, but when he realized what he'd done, and why, guilt had knifed him under the ribs. Now Matt knew what that was like.

"Hey, and I'm sorry I took off on you," Seth said. "I mean, you could have died out there."

Matt smiled. "In your shoes, I might have done the same. Forget it."

Seth hopped down from the stall board, reached for the stall latch, and clicked it open. "This is why I wanted you to come over," he said. "If you'll open that door," he pointed to the swinging door beyond Quest's stall.

"You mean . . . ," Matt said, eyebrows tilting inward. With a spiral, he tossed his football into a corner. A pitchfork clattered to the floor.

"Yup," Seth said. "I'd love to keep him, tame him, but

it's not best for Fudge. And look at him. He's better now, at least over the wound. He'll find food."

"And what about wolves?" Matt asked, facing him. "I mean, aren't you worried . . . ?"

"You said," Seth said, leaning against the stall door, "that if I really cared about wolves, then why wouldn't I let Fudge go, something like that. Well . . ." He paused, pulled his chapped lip in, ran his top teeth over the edge, and let it out again. "Sometimes, you have to let go. I want wolves, moose, all of it. But in order to have wilderness, I figure we can't control every part of it, and that includes Fudge." He paused. There he went again, spouting off like a brain-on-wheels. "Does that make sense?"

Matt grabbed a piece of hay from the stack of bales and stuck it in his mouth. "I don't know. Sometimes, you go over my head." He looked at Fudge. "But I know this. If he never leaves his stall, he'll never become the bull moose of some cow moose's dreams." He smiled at his own joke. "Y'know what I mean?"

"I get it," Seth said. "I'm not that much of an egghead."

"Oh, don't get me wrong. You're an egghead," Matt said, "but that's okay. I don't always let on, but some-

121

times I actually learn a few things from you."

Seth met his eyes and gave a nod. "Good."

Matt walked the length of the barn, opened the door until it jammed in the snow, then stood aside. "Ready!" he called.

Seth eased open the stall door. "Okay, Fudge," he said. The calf stopped rubbing and eyed the open gap.

"You're on your own now. Go out there and multiply."

Seth backed himself behind the stall door, and the calf stepped forward—one step, two. When it found itself in the walkway, it pawed, swung its head left and right, then trotted for the sunshine outside the door, leaving tear-shaped tracks in the dirt.

Seth ran a few yards behind it. "C'mon!" he called to Matt, who joined him in breaking through the deep snow after the moose calf.

The moose followed along the fence, then stopped abruptly beside a crab apple tree. It extended its rubbery lips and pulled a remaining dried apple into its mouth.

"There's more under the snow," Seth called.

For a moment, the moose calf looked toward him with its brown marble eyes, as if considering whether to stay or go. But it turned, lumbered off on its long legs, picking up speed as it headed for the thickest trees, and like a ghost stepping into another world, disappeared into the late afternoon shadows.

For a few minutes, the boys perched on the split rail fence, boots hooked on the bottom rung, watching. The silence between them was comfortable, the kind that comes from knowing someone a long time.

Matt spoke. "I think he's gone."

"Yeah, maybe," Seth answered, holding a hope the calf might return. One thing he knew. Moose—like wolves—were wild, part of a greater mystery he would never fully understand. And that was just fine.

He could live with that.

Author's Note

When this novel was first written, wolves were on the Endangered Species list. Their numbers were woefully low because of excessive bounty hunting and trapping. With protection, the wolf population successfully rebounded and was eventually "delisted" or removed from the list of threatened or endangered species. Now individual states determine how to "manage" their wolf populations.

In 2012, the state of Minnesota opened a hunting season on wolves. Each year, hunters are allowed to hunt or trap wolves until an overall "harvest," or number of wolves killed, is reached.

Without a doubt, the wolf will always be the focus of debate, arousing admiration and fear, love and hate. One thing is certain: the wolf has made a strong comeback from its threatened existence and again adds its song to the chorus of the land.

Further Reading About Wolves

Decade of the Wolf: Returning the Wild to Yellowstone (revised and updated edition), by Douglas W. Smith and Gary Ferguson (Lyons Press, 2012).

Face to Face with Wolves, by Jim Brandenburg (National Geographic Press, 2010).

Wolf Almanac: A Celebration of Wolves and Their World (revised edition), by Robert H. Busch (Lyons Press, 2007).

Wolf Empire: An Intimate Portrait of a Species, by Scott Ian Barry (Lyons Press, 2007).

Wolves, by Seymour Simon (HarperCollins, 2010).

Wolves: Behavior, Ecology, and Conservation, by David L. Mech (University of Chicago Press, 2007).

Mary Casanova is the author of more than thirty books for young readers, ranging from picture books such as *The Day Dirk Yeller Came to Town, Utterly Otterly Night,* and *One-Dog Canoe* to novels, including *Frozen* (Minnesota, 2012). Her books are on many state reading lists and have received the American Library Association Notable Book Award, Aesop Accolades from the American Folklore Society, Parents' Choice Gold Award, *Booklist* Editors' Choice, and two Minnesota Book Awards. She speaks frequently around the country at readings, schools, and libraries.

She lives with her husband and three dogs in a turn-of-the-century house in Ranier, Minnesota, near the Canadian border.